Don't Understand

Don't Understand

Paresh Bhandari

ZORBA BOOKS

ZORBA BOOKS

Published in India by Zorba Books, 2018

Website: www.zorbabooks.com
Email: info@zorbabooks.com

Copyright © Paresh Bhandari
Cover designed by Author Paresh Bhandari

ISBN: 978-93-87456-62-4
e book: 978-93-87456-63-1

Zorba Books Pvt. Ltd.(opc)
Gurgaon, INDIA

Printed at Repro Knowledgecast Limited, Thane

To

My Beloved Readers

(The Hunters of Excellence, Experience
and Expertise)

Contents

Acknowledgement

This work is dedicated to my *father*, author of many unpublished works; my *family, friends* and all the *folks* around me who gave me inspiration, insights and invitations to vivid experiences of life.

I am grateful for their company.

There are people who are fortunate or unfortunate to be much closer to me, whom I call *"Beloved Ones"*. They need a special mention here for their love because without love you don't have any motivation.

I am grateful for their care.

I have a very small and limited circle of beautiful and talented friends – those whom I tried to tie together into a revolutionary club – *"The Hunters"*. I wrote these articles for them and these were delivered to them in their mailboxes as *huntorials*. They had a passive, yet very important part in creating these *huntorials*, because without a listening consciousness there can't be a speaking consciousness.

I am grateful for their consciousness.

These chapters are slight modifications of those *huntorials* for those who are out of the circle, but may enter-in anytime they feel like.

You can't accomplish any creative work without support which may be active or passive, material or emotional. Support remains unseen but is a very valuable contribution. I got very kind support from *every person* whom I asked for it.

I am grateful for their contribution.

Last, but not the least my sincere thanks to *Dr. Vasant Joshi* who blessed me by writing an affectionate *Foreword* for this book with his experienced pen.

I am grateful for his creativity and compassion.

Foreword

I am very happy to write this Foreword for the fact that this book presents multiple dimensions of Life and Living. As acknowledged by the author, the work is "inspired" by the contemporary enlightened mystic, Osho, "from the space of love and meditation" – as the two sources that the author feels indebted to. The author has indeed covered a wide range of thoughts and issues very effectively and has made it relevant for the times we are living now.

Somewhere deep down in man there is fear of nature. That fear of nature has created many problems. It has created an ugly civilization, a rotten culture, an anti-nature technology, a science against ecology, a religion which is not in tune with your innermost being. It is time for man to revolt against all this that has happened to humanity in the past and continues to happen today!

We watch our physical health and through a set of established economic indicators, we also worry about the health of our economy. However, by contrast, we hardly care for our spiritual health. We find, in dismay, alienation, violence, exploitation, pollution and many such de-humanizing factors. We urgently need to recognize, as the author feels, that we need to do pioneering work in designing a spiritual index that can show at which rate mankind is making or destroying lives.

It is precisely in this very context that the following appeal by the learned scholar becomes so meaningful: "My message for the students and learners is to minimize on probability and maximize on potential so that the possibility of success gets optimized....Learn and experiment to open up the possibilities of understanding and experience."

According to Dr. Erminia Guarneri, medical director of the Scripps Ornish Program at the Scripps Foundation for Medicine and Science, "We have to look beyond the physical healing. We have to take a look at the whole person because the mental, emotional and even the spiritual aspects of healing cannot be separated from the physical." Life flows between polarities such as movement and rest, action and let go, between tension and being at ease, using and regaining energy. With this understanding, meditation is seen as a process which enables the individual to adjust oneself effectively to changing situations at different levels of one's life and living conditions.

The contemporary enlightened mystic, Osho reminds us: "One creates one's essence every moment – how one lives, how one speaks, how one moves. Only an individual is responsible for creating essence, no one else. Giving essence, giving true meaning to life, is the greatest challenge and the uppermost responsibility. Not just what we know matters, how we use what we know, how we incorporate it in enhancing the quality and meaning of life, matters even more. What this implies is that, 'I am not only part of the problem; I am part of the solution too"'. This is what Osho points out as the evolutionary process – responsibility and awareness, vision and action.

I congratulate and commend Paresh Bhandari for his excellent presentation of ideas with a sense of urgency giving the reader an opportunity to reflect upon the significantly important areas of our life and living for one's own understanding and experiment.

Dr. Vasant Joshi
(Swami Satya Vedant)
Ph.D. University of Michigan, USA
M.A., Ph.D., M.S. University of Baroda, India

Reader's Note

Reading a book doesn't make a reader. The real reader doesn't read the book; he reads the author through the book. Book just remains a medium for him to reach the author.

Those who know Osho and have read him or listened to him, will find at many places as if Osho is speaking to them. Yes, the inspiration behind these words is Osho and these are coming from the space of *love* and *meditation* – the two mystical arts that I learned from him.

With gratefulness for his grace, I am sharing this space with my readers. What follows is an invitation to enter and enjoy this space.

You are most welcome!

Prologue

On 25th Nov, 2004 it was my fortune or misfortune to be at one of the most reputed medical institute in the country. My father was getting discharged after his right side bi-inguinal hernia surgery and left hydrocele. And the same day, the non-medical staff of the hospital was on strike because a 14-year old child of one staff member had died because of doctor's negligence or carelessness whatsoever.

We were waiting to leave that God-forsaken place as their dues with us and our dues with them including some surgical stuff were to be cleared but the payment counter was close due to strike. One lady in our ward made a remark for my father that he was very lucky to have a son of "Shravan Kumar" model. And my mother couldn't stop adding that the son was very cool (tolerant!).

But my mother's statement became contradictory (not for me, I'll explain later) when after a few hours the staff members resumed their work. We paid our dues and asked the Sister (not mine) of the ward to return our unused surgical stuff (it was almost half of what we had submitted, as surgery of both the sides could not be performed). The Sister humiliated my mother and passed comments not expected from a responsible person.

And it took seconds for the cool son to become HOT and it took an hour and great effort on my mother's part to bring me to my COOL state. The lady who had stolen my originality by calling me "Shravan Kumar" was greatly shocked and asked me "You were so cool (fool), what happened to you?" I just smiled and didn't explain anything to her because she couldn't have UNDERSTOOD. No, no the secret is that I am not a good speaker, but a very good writer.

It is this skill of mine that prompted me to write this series of articles. Before I explain the basic principles of nature, first thing first: *"Never make your judgments on any person, because you can only judge acts which collectively make a person"* (e.g. my acts that created a CONTRADICTION like me).

What I have understood are two basic principles of Nature: **Relativity** and **Antagonism**. If we go further, there is one ultimate principle and that principle states there is no place for principles in primordial Nature or alternatively, primordial Nature is not guided by any principle.

Principle of Relativity: Nothing is absolute in nature, not even Time and Space. Then everything must be relative. That means if I am cool, I am cool with respect to persons who are hotter.

Principle of Antagonism: For every action, there is equal and opposite reaction. That means if I am cool, I have great potential to become hot.

Now, as I previously told "I am not a good speaker but a very good writer". That means I am not as good in speaking as others are, but I am better than them in writing. Also there is chance and possibility when I can speak as a good speaker, but lose my writing skill. I can't lose my writing skill if I don't have it.

Even when there was a lot of tension at hospital, I was able to get relief by stealing some moments of *hunting* with my "*Hunting Eyes*", the victims being the beautiful nurses over there. Can you now understand me when I say "I am very optimistic"?

.....

Yes, you are right, but you may be wrong....

Wonderful: Relativity and *Antag*onism...

Keep Reading. You may understand or may not, but I accept both cases..

Yours accurately,
The Author

Donate Blood, Expand Yourself

I say

"DON'T UNDERSTAND"
Because in trying to *understand*,
You may *misunderstand!*

Chapter One

Change

Nothing is permanent except change. The nature itself is ever-changing but the minds of the vast majority of insincere people oppose any change. They criticize the person practicing change in his physical grooming or dressing style and condemn him as carrying unstable mind. But believe me, intelligent minds are always unstable. They don't agree with what they think a day before and that's how they improve and refine themselves to bring a revolution.

Being sincere does not mean being serious. A serious person may not be sincere at all. Sincerity means living each moment completely while seriousness often is holding back, being stiff when time invites you to change and rejoice. Serious people often close themselves and their minds inside cages and walls allowing in only air to breath. That is the only change in their lives. They don't laugh or smile because that may change the look of their faces. The serious people never appreciate a joke, but they laugh when they should not.

Once such people were invited by King Janak for some serious discussion on life, philosophy, spirituality etc. Astavakra was not invited, but he came, knowing there was some scope to learn, to change. But as he entered, the learned people there started laughing on the typical movements of his eight cornered body.

Astavakra told King Janak "I came without being invited because I thought something sincere concerning the subjectivity of human being was being discussed but now it seems people here have nothing to do with soul. They can't see beyond this body. And it were better if I hadn't come because it is not a group of learned people but a group of cobblers who are interested in skin and identify person by his body. I had come to share my ideas but now it seems useless. These insincere people seem to have understood me from my body structure."

We may seem to be a structure from outside but from inside we are much more – a helix of revolution.

Really Astavakra!
Happy Change..., Happy Reading.......

Discover Yourself

Chapter Two

Gandhi

*T*here are some people in this world that you want to spit on their face. You become so helpless before them; they fill you with inferiority. You either crucify them or kill them. Jesus and Gandhi are such people – so true to themselves. It was the time of Gandhi's influence over whole of India, when one mother took her son to him, so that Gandhi could motivate him to give up eating too much of jaggery. But Gandhi himself used to take a lot of jaggery, so he refused and asked her to come after two weeks. He didn't ask the boy to give up jaggery before he himself succeeded in giving it up.

This is one of the greatest talismans, Gandhi has given to the world – greater than his philosophy of non-violence – "*Before doing any act to the other, put yourself in his place.*" You practice this and you will find non-violence automatically appearing in your life. But beware! Don't do it with food because then you would never be able to satisfy your appetite.

3

Gandhi experimented a lot on truth, but in this world nothing is 100 percent true. Things are either 90% true or one from the truth pair or they are altogether false or fiction or a limiting case.

If I say – "*Naveen is a man.*",
my statement is a limiting case of the statement:
"Naveen is a human being."

If I say – "*Truth wins.*",
my statement is a fiction because I may have read many stories where the winner is proved to be true. The reality is different:
"Strength wins whether true or false and weakness always loses."

If I say – "*World is full of sorrow.*",
my statement is one from the truth pair because
"World is full of joy."
is also true.

Most of our statements are usually false like –
"*I love you.*"
"*You are my friend.*"
"*You are intelligent.*"
"*You are beautiful.*"

Beauty and intelligence speak for themselves, we don't have to declare.

We should rejoice that Gandhi experimented with Truth and Non-Violence because we are also experimenting.......with Life. Results of Gandhi's experiments are his privacy and are only for him. When learning from Gandhi – '*to experiment*', we should discover, accept and preserve our own results, not bothering about Gandhi's results.

Experiment and Experience Truth, Awareness and Bliss!
Happy Experimenting..., Happy Reading.......

Know Truth, Know Bliss

Chapter Three

Rise

*O*nce, I was with my friends and I counted. I found that Ears were double the number of Mouths. I quickly reached conclusion and started reciting my self-composed poetry. There was applause and I came to know that the clapping hands were also twice the number of mouths. This whole phenomenon has inspired me to proceed with the recital of my thoughts, not with mouth but with a pen to my new but more mature friends, knowing again that there are good minds to listen and open hearts to clap.

Marriages had been a hot topic for me during my late twenties and early thirties that sometimes I attended, sometimes I was proposed for and sometimes I was the advised and even the adviser. Some of my gallant friends who have great regard for fair sex, used to say – "Never reject any girl and if you don't like or want to go for the holy-tie, make that she rejects you instead." (Were they inspired by ideals shown in movies and dramas?) I have also heard that "True love never tends to marriage and if it does, consider that the end is near and the female is more dominating."

Marriages are made in heaven but so are love, divorce, thunder, storms and rains. I feel marriage itself is an arrangement with future requirements of understanding, compromise and adjustments. But we often hear terms like 'Love Marriage' and 'Arranged Marriage' which gives the notion that love marriage is all together a different thing. In my opinion love marriage is a subset and a small scale 'arranged marriage' where the required arrangements are done by the couple concerned without involving their families in the process, particularly as initiators or decision-makers. Love marriages approved by families become 'arranged love marriages'.

Love marriage takes less time to occur because maturity, planning and thoughts are not required. *I love the girl and accept her as my life partner and don't bother whether my family likes her or not, accepts her or not.* Chances are that these may not be stable due to lack of experience and involvement of experienced people in decision making, who would have taken into account more logical things than love, to decide whether the match is long-lasting and rigid.

Arranged marriage takes more time to occur because each and every member of the family with different likes/ dislikes/ prejudices/ criteria/ expectations/ superstitions etc. needs to be satisfied. Horoscope matching and sometimes totally unimportant and unnecessary issues spring up and need to be solved. Then there is an evil often associated with arranged marriages – the issue of dowry. The bigger the family, the more the issues and the more the delay in marriage. *Let them find a girl who is the best golden mean of their choices, and then I will try to recall what I like and want in my life partner.* Gifts are not tailor-made but sometimes they just fit.

Naturally the outcome of arranged marriage is more stability – why not, who wants to lose something gained after long struggle and when you know you are not competent in arranging love marriage.

There is a third category called 'Forced Marriage' wherein the family applies pressure and forces the marriage on the victim (mostly girls but sometimes boys too), taking into account only its own choices and parameters. And sometimes vice versa happens. The family has to bow down before the strong bond of love between the couples.

Love marriages are mostly inter-caste marriages and arranged marriages are often intra-caste or caste dependent. But can't arranged marriages be made inter-caste or in other words can't we arrange inter-caste or inter-religious marriages? If we can do that, many of our social and national problems, which are tried to be solved through other approaches, will get solved. Communalism will automatically die and we will find ourselves in more truly integrated India – a nation not integrated as a need through speeches and patriotic songs. This may lead to the need of more integrity and we may like to experiment with 'International Marriages' (what about inter-planetary marriages?). Foreign policies will become relations. Nationality will disappear and internationality will appear. Then there won't be any Friend or Enemy nations, but nations of Father, Maternal nations and nations of In-Laws. Would then there be any possibility of war or economic disparities or technological divides?

But for that we need to think and need to **Rise, Raise and Race.** At last I would say – "*Rise* beyond all Divides so that you can *raise* your fellows to feel what pleasure it gives. And if you've really risen, you will certainly *raise* so that there is someone on your grounds to *race* with you so that you reach your Goal of Excellence as the best record".

Happy Rising..., Happy Reading.......

No Tobacco, No Blood Pollution

Chapter Four

Study

People talk about friends and enemies, categorize as friends and enemies. But do you think that people are friends or enemies? The people you come across in life are either fellows or rivals. Both your fellows and rivals need you because you share the same goal or destination with them. They travel with you. Then what is the difference?... Between a fellow and a rival. Both are in your team, both learn from you and teach you. The difference is – the fellow enjoys the journey with you and also enjoys sharing the goal with you; while the rival travels with you towards the goal, but when the destination comes closer he throws you out. He shares the journey, but he doesn't want to share the goal. He wants it all, alone. Fellow says:-

> Let's go you and I
> To claim whole sky,
> I'll claim one half
> You claim the other half.

What does a rival say – you can make out.

Think about it. Are your classmates your class-fellows or exam-rivals; roommates your room partners or room dividers; your colleagues fellow participants or competitors?

Once, one of my students asked me. Students may also be your rivals – 'rivalry for knowledge'. Once they have gained from you and more from other sources, they get equipped to show you down. But this one was a fellow and he asked me "How much should I study?" My reply was "You shouldn't study, you should try to learn. Then it doesn't matter how long it takes. It may take the whole day or a few hours."

Study is nothing but a pressure (from parents, teachers), a show to your fellows and rivals that you are working hard. You may sit for long hours just keeping the book open or turning its pages – grasping or learning nothing. Study may become an acting of learning. Learning doesn't need hard work; it is an outcome of your curiosity. And study may become only one of the ways of learning. That study no more remains quantitative, it becomes qualitative.

You learn to earn – a reward, a degree or cracking an exam. Then you forget.

You learn, you forget;
The more you learn, the more you forget.

Then why do you learn? To hide your stupidity. This is not true learning. True learning means you've understood. Now there is no fear of forgetting. When you've understood, there is no need to learn. Now you can teach. You are no more a student, you become a teacher.

And if you are learning something that you understand or know, then you either misunderstand or want to remain a learner. Remember learning may not always be understanding, as study may not always be learning. When there is understanding, there is no learning, there is teaching. Then you only learn how to teach.

Newton knows gravity, Einstein understands relativity. By developing theories and formula, they are not learning these phenomenon. They are only learning how to explain. As time progresses, their formula may prove wrong or just a limiting case, but that doesn't mean that they hadn't understood. Rather they couldn't address new curiosities and queries in their explanations.

You can give up learning and study, and feel that you understand and know all. No, that won't solve the purpose. Instead, to understand, you should try to learn – not just for learning but to understand. Because only when you are ready to learn, you are ready for understanding. And how to learn? "Study" – because study is the fastest way to learn. And when you study, study to learn. If you don't find yourself as learning, stop your study.

Once you can do this, then study becomes both learning and understanding.

And study should be a tribute to the past; to the learned, to those who understood, and collected and compiled for you what they learnt. It should be thankfulness to their hard work and devotion that relieved you of reinventing the wheel.

Differences in understanding create gaps among people, which we know as generation gaps. These gaps divide people into young and old, married and unmarried, father and son. Father has more experience which the son lacks and father has forgotten that once he was also a son. Experiences enhance your understanding but experiences never come from teachings. Teachings just stimulate you to experiment and it is experiment that yields experience. But the married ones try to teach the unmarried in a hope to share their experience.

The old are always teaching the young to act according to them without letting them experiment and follow all levels of experiences that happened to them. When young, they acted the same way for lack of experience but now they want their children to experience in short cut from their teachings. The children don't understand because they don't have experience and they are energetic enough to experiment and want to experience at their own. What they want to experience seems useless to the old because they forget that it is the stair towards the useful that the old are experiencing. This confusion altogether results in total opposition of the old. The young may just act to agree with them from outside, but they disagree from the inside. And this is their respect, which may sometimes become disrespect also. But both respect and disrespect come out of generation gap.

Any experiment is your effort and experience is your effortlessness. And when effortlessness follows effort, you achieve. The experienced people are reversing the process. They are asking the youth to be effortless, to sit quiet and listen. And they want the youth to act or make effort, once they gain knowledge from elder's experiences. But what you gain from others is not yours; the only thing that is yours is your achievement. And achievement comes from the magical combination of effort and effortlessness – do, wait...do and wait. So learn how to balance, how to write the notes of effort and effortlessness to get the beautiful composition, called achievement. Remember effort alone will not give you success – to succeed you also need to be receptive and you become receptive when you are effortless.

My message for the students and learners is to minimize on probability and maximize on potential so that the possibility of success gets optimized. You are born to succeed and achieve. Success and achievement are your potential; you just have to harness them. Don't make them probabilities by studying and not learning. Learn and experiment to open up the possibilities of understanding and experience.

Probability becomes possibility if effort is added and possibility converts into potential when effortlessness is added. And potential is nothing but hidden success.

If the message is clear to the learners, it will be clear to the teachers too, as one is effort and the other effortlessness and there is no generation gap. There is full potential, no need to calculate probability or study possibility.

Happy Learning..., Happy Reading.......

They Say...
What They Say..
Let Them Say.

Chapter Five

Community Crysis

*C*ommunities arise with the slogan of unity, but end up as instruments of rivalry. The reasons cited behind the formation of any community are security, strength, achievement and common interests. In majority, we feel secure; and with community, we are not alone.

Equality and similarity in strength, resources, interests, goals, religion, region and social position inspire a group of people to initiate the formation of another label for themselves besides name, by which they like themselves to be called and using which they gather to achieve or do what they can't as an individual. Security is the basic reason for the most common man to join any community. So the larger the community, the more is the security. And those in minority suffer, the greatest sufferers being those who don't believe in any community and respect their individuality. They are bombarded and exploited by almost anybody, if they don't know fighting or common clever tactics of survival and struggle. Sometimes they can even become victims of community politics (rivalry among various communities) if they carry the potential or eligibility for membership of any particular community/communities, but are not members.

But as an individual, a person is less insecure than as member of a community and when a community member falls prey, he finds not a single person but a whole mad mob against him and not only him but his whole family. And it comes to kill for reasons that are sometimes unknown to him and for faults for which he is not responsible. He has to suffer for each and every deed of his fellows or the whole community, besides his own. Moreover, he faces another spontaneous exploitation, internal to community, against which he can't even resist as long as he is part of the community. This exploitation is imposed by those few people who founded or initiated these nuisances for their personal vested interests in the guise of servers of the weak or who sprang up as leaders and soon took hold and control of all activities and decision making of the community. These so-called servers are the main beneficiaries and whatever little benefits others get, are at the cost of mental slavery. The invisible, falsely created organism called community swallows the real, visible individual.

The real entity – the individual seems to disappear but never disappears. Each action is performed in the name of community but is for the self. Modern man is clever, educated in an uneducated way. His uneducated part becomes the member of the community, but the educated part tries best to reap the benefits of membership in his own interests. Therefore, everyone whether the exploiter or the exploited knows that there is nobody like community, and works for self-benefit. He always thinks of exploiting the others. 'Better', 'survival', 'anyhow' are his keywords. The word 'sacrifice' is still used, but sacrifice has got buried deep in history. Not that sacrifices don't occur – but nobody sacrifices, only compels or makes others to sacrifice. Everybody is to exploit the community and the others inside and outside, through it. The result is that man's selfishness gets beautifully covered by the intelligently tailored clothes of community.

Man is a unit and humanity is unity. Unity is achieved when the unit is destroyed or in positive terminology, when unit is taken as part of unity. Creating bigger units like community does not create unity; bigger units create bigger rivalries. The bigger the rivalry, the greater is the destruction. The potential of destruction is the greatest when the rivalry touches the national level. We create communities, and then we talk of harmony – communal harmony; as if harmony were a communal phenomenon. As long as communities exist, harmony can't. Harmony needs a living source; the individual is the source and the non-living communities destroy the individual. Harmony can exist between individuals and unity is achieved not at community level but at the unit level.

For unity, units need to interact, not their commonality, and community is commonality. And when communities interact, that interaction is bound to be based on that which is uncommon. This interaction if positive can only complement, not harmonize. Some communities are found to exist at ease with each other; they are just complementing each other and that too is short-lived, depending on the situation and other surrounding factors. Harmony is achieved only by the dissolution of the two. Not community, humanity is the ultimate harmony that can exist among humans.

Community is the collection of individuals and harmony is the connection among them. Connection is possible, but individuals can't be collected because nobody can collect. This is the limitation that we can't collect or meet the other because we have boundaries; but we can connect to anybody infinitely and forever. So our endeavor should be to connect individually to persons, not to any groups or communities. While connecting we should concentrate on the person, his frequency and try to match it with ours. We should forget his caste, creed and community. If we don't know, we should avoid asking, if it is not necessary.

Through connecting and matching frequencies, soon we find that we have somehow given birth to an interest group. This interest group is not to fulfill our personal or financial interests, but to share our mental, artistic, intellectual and emotional interests, and to support and groom each other's creativity and ideas. Those who are not part of your group are not your enemies, but your neighbours. As soon as an interest group marches towards being a community, it is better to have it dissolved.

Bill Clinton has said that there are two types of people in the world: those who have seen the Taj and those who haven't. In the same way there may be two kinds of people in your life: those you have connected to and those you have yet to. So it is not that someone belongs to your group and someone does not. It is only that someone is still unconnected and that connection is being tried. You are still on the way to harmony with humanity. One point is to be remembered that connection is not a relation. Relation is rigid, but connection keeps changing. When connection is given a name, it acquires rigidity and becomes a relation. It is your choice to name a connection or un-name a relation or keep changing the name of connection or following connection-disconnection-connection. But in my opinion, naming limits; hides the reality and feel; and destroys the beauty of a connection.

Osho has proposed and coined a term called 'commune'. It has got its definition here or it can be defined here. Commune contains those people with whom you have a connection, not a single connection but ever changing connections that are getting intense and deeper, that are spreading in all dimensions. Probably he also means the same. Commune is a way to harmony with humanity and it is the best substitute to community. Commune is the un-naming and the destruction of community; it is a droplet of humanity.

In commune, you can disconnect and be alone whenever you like to; because you are not needed against anybody or for a war or for shouting slogans. And you can again connect, whenever you feel like; you are always most welcome. Sometimes you are alone and sometimes you are part of it. And when you are part of it, you are part of all communes.

Man can't live alone and live with continuously. Therefore he joins or forms a community, where he feels he is not alone, but can remain always disconnected, to fulfill his own interests. Out of these two needs of being with a group, he joins a community; and of being alone he establishes rivalry with other communities. Also a man can't live with the same people continuously; hence he switches between family and his community. A couple is delighted when some of their friends or folks visit their house. This gives them a break from continuous togetherness.

Family is also a small community or is it not? In most families, there are no connections but relations which are very professional and based on expectations and performance. Like in offices, there is a boss called father and other performers like wife and roles like son. The first community a child encounters in his life is his family while he searches for a commune and love all the time. Can a family become a commune? Yes, if relations can be converted into love. Then the whole structure of the family will change and lose its rigidity. There will be young families with two-three couples living together; there may be families of old people who have decided to live together rather than living with their sons, who are on the faster track of life. Some people would be parenting the sons of their friends while some sons would be living with their uncles. The community nature of family will dissolve. There can't be any rivalry between families of young and olds as both are pursuing different suitable paths. The younger will uninterruptedly earn, learn and progress while the old will be able to live peacefully in worship and sharing their experience.

But before the conversion of family, the person needs to be converted. Today each single person has become his community or we have made him so. We address a person by his community like 'Bengali', 'Whites', 'Negro', 'Texan' etc., if he is below us and can tolerate. We've afforded to know his community, can't we find his name? Before asking name we ask him about his community. We don't like to call persons by their names even if we know; we prefer to use surnames to remind them of their community. By connecting a person to a community we think we can know, identify and assess him better in no time. This is because we don't know how to know; otherwise every person carries his identity in his face, words and actions, and can be assessed by his thoughts.

In Maharashtra, they won't rent their house to a person from a particular part of India. Now they even don't want him to be seen in markets, streets and trains of Maharashtra. Brahman Sabha searches for a brilliant Brahmin student to provide scholarship, even if others are above and more intelligent than him. They want a pure Brahmin surname; if the surname is not in their list, they withdraw. When Arshad comes, you are attacked by Pakistan.

When we meet a Jew, we feel envious or dominated. This planet has witnessed many massacres and history has recorded the killing of millions of innocent people for the sake of killing a community. Only persons get killed, community never because community doesn't exist physically. It doesn't exist inside persons; instead persons exist inside this illusion, this crisis. This way of identification can be stopped, like name can be snatched from a person. Community of a person should not be taken as his identity. Then only community will vanish, killing is not required. Crashing the community by forgetting it is needed.

We go to a Hindu and we dominate or try to convert him. A person is dying of hunger and you are changing his name. This won't do. A person is illiterate and you are changing his books. He will feel insecure, irritated and frustrated. New communities are created to renovate the old but they just replace them. Communities are planned to transform humanity, but they take away the peace of life. Communities are created for the final holy war but they add terror to the minds of people. They create more wars; and wars create more communities. And the two fall in a vicious circle.

There is another seasonal phenomena associated with communities due to the existence of governing bodies, laws and the idea of social justice. It occurs in hundreds of years, when some particular communities are found to be lagging behind, exploited to poverty by other communities and losing resourcefulness and race of life. Then for social justice, laws are made and promotional schemes are introduced for this particular class of communities, inflicting injustice on others. The result does not improve the social scenario and the society in its sum total remains the same. Only a reversal is seen with the upper becoming the lower and the lower becoming the upper, maintaining the balance of numbers of haves and have-nots. Rather a little chaos is introduced – as 'the upper' never descends easily and resists; while it is unusual and unknown to 'the lower' to play 'the upper'. It is like promoting girls and finding that boys are getting demoralized. Some countries are thinking of reversing this girl-boy promotion scheme owing to the new results.

Then how can we survive with communities and how to face this crisis. Beware whenever you feel, politics is being played in the name of community; be alert and you can easily recognize the age-old 'divide and rule' policy. You are gaining popularity, earning fame; you are doing and performing better and people can be turned against you by turning them against your community. People are told to be beware of you and you are declared that community. All communities – the society may unite against you by uniting against your community. Your response is important; don't get aroused. Remarks against community hurt more than remarks against the person; because you are not responsible and you can't do anything. Don't follow the opponent; you remain on the individual level. Talk, solve, understand and make the other person understand at the individual level – that is reality. Don't drift from reality and be responsible for yourself only.

Whenever you encounter communal problems, don't fan the fire; don't initiate or support rumours. Instead try to dig out whose personal interests are initiating the madness. Understand, explain the real cause, educate people and hit at the root.

If you can't follow and understand all this, then follow my friend. He is the member of all communities. He is enjoying all the advantages and is safe unless he meets two communities simultaneously. Then he has to vanish. He is following fuzzy logic and everybody has such features and properties that he can claim membership of all communities. You can sit with women by saying that you also don't have beard and moustache. But the real trouble arises when all communities want their share from you and propose to divide you.

You might also find yourself in such trouble. By religion you are in one community, by social-regional-directional divisions and family names in another; and by profession, wealth, age and gender etc. in yet another.

When my friend found himself being dragged in all directions, he came to me and said "I want to be loyal; I want to be with one community. Hence I want to join your community". I said that I had never joined my community. He said "Then constitute one and join it". I told him that I was not in favour of any community and that he should better join some other community. He asked which community he should join.

I advised him to join his own community. He wondered what his community was. If one is not a human being, then he is either horse or donkey or lion etc. and he should remain in his community. When he discovers the human being inside, then he has to come out, because a true and intelligent human can't belong to community. But if a donkey leaves his community and joins that of horses, there is no gain. Rather he suffers great losses. The donkeys now no longer entertain him and what can the horses do with him. He can just be an entertainment for the horses, when they are at leisure. He can't run with them. What if a horse joins the community of donkeys? Then either he is not a horse or he wants to be a donkey. Still he will be alone; the donkeys will use him as a trademark outside and inside as a sink of their frustration. He won't make any improvement anywhere – in himself or his donkey fellows. The donkeys will say that even horses join their community, but will always remain donkeys.

In friendship, you forget community and whenever you are reminded, bitterness starts engulfing your friendship. In marriages and match-making you try to remember. Free your mind from community crisis, because it has started crying; free yourself in friendship; and get free into friendliness. There is crisis inside and outside communities; friendliness has no inside or outside – only calmness, pleasure and caring.

Keep hunting for friends…, Happy Friendship……!

Come…Come….
Let There be Coming…….
But No Community and No Oaths
of Communal Harmony!

Chapter Six

Interest Group

At this stage it is my pleasure as well as necessary to share what I want and try to explain below.

The Group:

The group should be committed to harness the creativity and thrill of the wonderful persons who constitute it. It should welcome innovative ideas and the quality of sharing, and provide help to its members. It should be an open forum for mutual advice, counselling and information interchange. It should have a revolutionary name. The members should take life as an experiment and keep on experimenting with various facets of life.

The group should believe in "Unite and Rule" rather than "Divide and Conquer". The members are not to impress, but to influence lives to make people multi-dimensionally orientated.

The Mission:

The group should have a mission (it should be propagated.......) of cleaning all that is dirty, giving up all that is obsolete, welcoming all that is new and innovative, producing and maintaining all that is worthwhile, and killing all that is evil. One should know that mottoes should die, once they get fulfilled. This provides chance for new mottoes and missions to be discovered that gives a new orientation to the group.

It looks contradictory but it is true that a goal must be given up when it gets fulfilled. If your motto is to remove poverty, you should remove poverty so that there is no need for such a motto again. But if you act as a motto-oriented person, you would never let your motto die and for that you would again generate poverty. This is what is happening in politics. Politicians create new parties with new mottoes, say for example, "*Motto of uniting humanity*", but they know that for the survival of their motto and their party, and hence their own survival, people should remain divided. Therefore, they act antagonistically talking of 'Unity' and working for 'Division of Society'.

The group should work differently, knowing that life is an experiment and everybody learns something through living. Then why not share experiences with like-minded people.

The Evolution:

The group takes time to evolve; it should continue to evolve, experimenting on 'Co-operation' and finding out if it really generates strength. We can feel the power of 'Information' in our time. That means the members should keep each other well informed if they find that the information is of benefit to the other. This sharing of information should be practiced frequently – information that is of benefit, yet the other is unaware of.

The group should always be grateful for the interest and kind response of its members. But nothing can be declared good or bad about the group. This is the job of others who stand and watch outside the group. There should not be any claim that the group is good. This is because there are no definitions of 'good' and 'bad' and if there are, those keep changing with time, place, situations, communities and cultures. Moreover such declarations lead to conclusion that means "THE END". And the group should not be the end but a beginning – the birth of a child. It has to grow without any prejudices of good and bad.

Rather than focusing on conclusions and nurturing prejudices, the group should aim at striving to construct opinions based on facts and reality. The group should respect the opinions and ideas of its members and these should be the most important to the group. The three Cs – *Comparison*, *Competition* and *Condemnation* must be circumvented as much as can be.

The Structure:

It would be better if the group is an un-chaired one with a core team of members (founders and re-founders) providing valuable suggestions, ideas and *creative* criticism regularly. It should not be a one-man club. The pioneer person may be invisible because "Wonders occur when the person becomes *invisible* and his ideas start becoming *visible*". The source of all ideas is Nature's Intellect; ideas just land on some mind – ready to receive and accept. The zeal inside the group can be created by constant support and benevolent suggestions from its members who work invisibly and survive the group to its reputed status.

The group can even be in virtual domains; that has its own immeasurable pleasure. Virtuality and invisibility create beauty, but nothing hides and there is full transparency. To bring all *members* of group on a common physical platform, activities and initiatives can be taken by the members, especially *Founder Members* and the core team. Some good and well-planned excursions may be organized and coordinated with wonderful themes in and around the Headquarters of the Club. The success of the group can't be one person's effort; it should have everyone's participation. For total participation in the activities of the group, all members must be invited and given chance to express their views.

The Idea:

The group should think beyond persons and take the help of literature and ideas for the transformation of mind and hence life. The language of the group may be formal or informal, personal or impersonal, bookish or non-bookish. To convey something in writing, you need to be bookish or in today's world of Internet, may be e-bookish. Communication, not language is important for the group.

The goal of the group is to tell that goals are not destination. Sometimes they become stations to your destination and at others they may become the greatest limitations. If Leonardo da Vinci's goal were to become an engineer (which is the goal of millions of people today) we won't have the world's greatest genius who was an engineer too.

Helping, rising, sharing, enjoying, feeling light, celebrating, cooperating, informing and spreading a revolution of transformation towards improvement with a scientific aptitude of experimentation is what *The Group* must stand for. Group interactions may be excellent or poor, but these should be much awaited, worth pondering and sharing, and should provoke such thoughts, which trigger useful actions.

So let's experiment by helping and influencing each other and accept the results with a truly scientific mind.

The group may be family, office, society, school, health club or regular gathering.

Keep Experimenting..., Keep Reading.......

To Err is Humane...
And not to Err is Inhumane...

Chapter Seven

Don't Understand

Sorry to disturb you, busy people. But it's necessary for me to share some pleasure, some humour and some nonsense with you. What prompted me for this is the phrase "NOT THAT" which I received through email from one person, writing "I am not THAT person". This has popped up many events on the screen of my mind. Some of these are real and some just from my dreams and imaginations.

I am not differentiating between these events because I feel there is no difference between dreams and reality. Reality is nothing but a deeper, denser and longer dream tied logically. Similarly a lie is nothing but truth distorted or in hidden form.

I START my narration (please digest):

3) One day I went to my friend. I was shocked because all his relatives and neighbours were mourning at the death of his twin brother. My friend was drunk; he rested his head on my shoulder and started remembering his brother. He told that his brother was always benefitted and for whole life took the credit of good jobs done by my friend. He said "When I helped someone, he was patted on the back and when he teased some girl, I was the one to get a beating. But today he has compensated for all that. I had died and the people took his corpse."

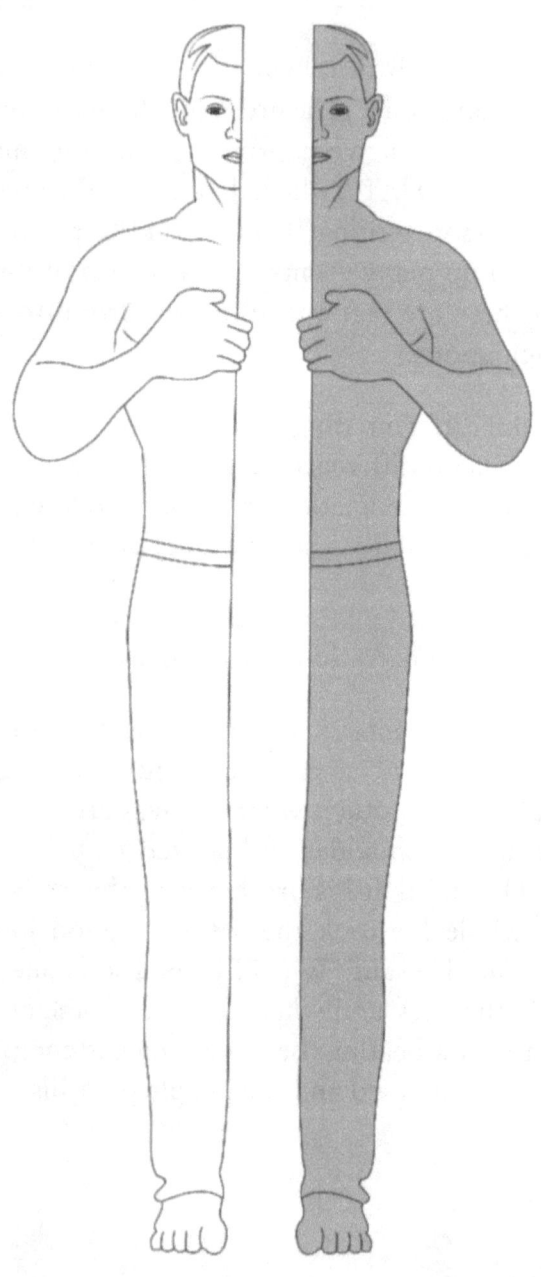

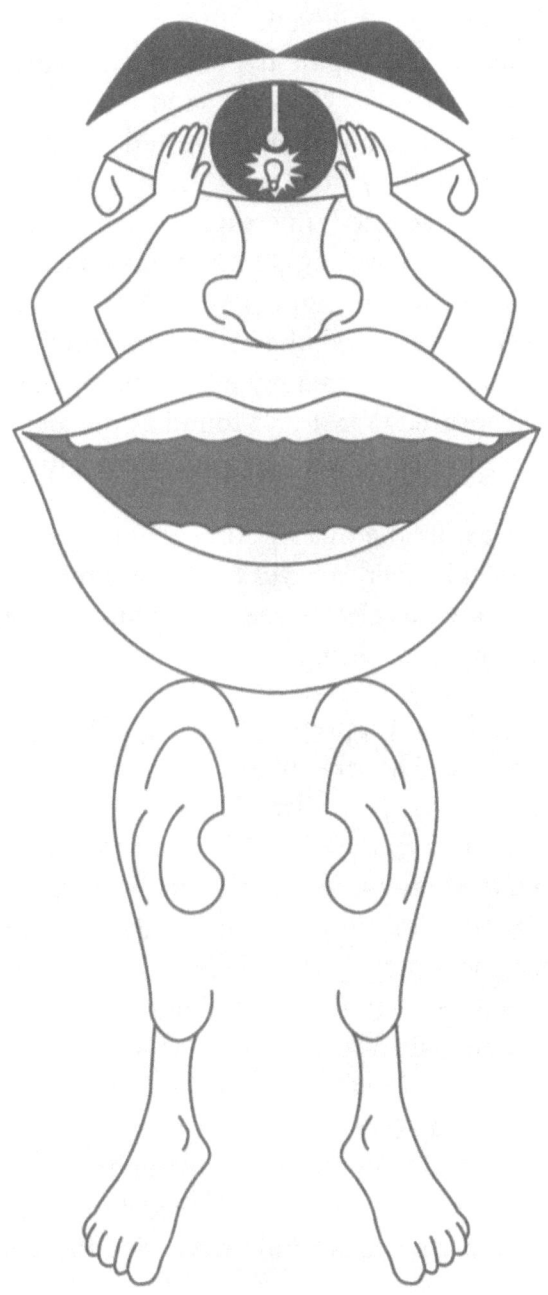

1) When I was a child, one question always disturbed me – which is the organ by which we can see (and differentiate between "THAT" and "NOT THAT"). I decided to harness my intelligence and use my scientific temper. I covered my nose with my hands – I was still seeing; then I covered my ears, everything was still visible. I tried by covering all my organs, but there was no obstruction to my sight. I was disappointed. Then suddenly, I remembered that I had forgotten to cover my eyes. I quickly covered my eyes with my hands – the vision disappeared. Yes, I had found at the age of three, through experiment that it is eye through which we see.

But today, at the age of forty I am again puzzled, because when I cover my eyes I still see something. Even when I sleep, I can clearly see the dreams. So my quest to find the organ of seeing still continues.

7) When I was 15, preparing for my Xth Board I went to sleep at 12 AM one night. I again started seeing (organ unknown). Two aliens from another planet took me from my bed to their UFO. There I found they were going to use Mem-Tame rays to extract all my memory to their typical machine (scientifically motivated like me). I became worried – how would I face exams, how would I recognize my friends and family. I thought "Do we memorize just to forget someday, do we live just to die someday." As I was thinking, I saw the alien doctor putting some cap-like instrument over my skull. I was horrified and suddenly I woke up to find my mother who was trying to wake me up. I was saved, but my memory! I quickly wrote some formula on paper and compared

to my NCERT book. My memory was fine, but why was the lady beside my bed looking at me amazingly.

10) Once I slept on the sofa in my drawing room. Again, though my eyes were closed, I started seeing myself, sleeping in my bedroom with my cat. When I woke up, I was really sleeping in my bedroom. How come!

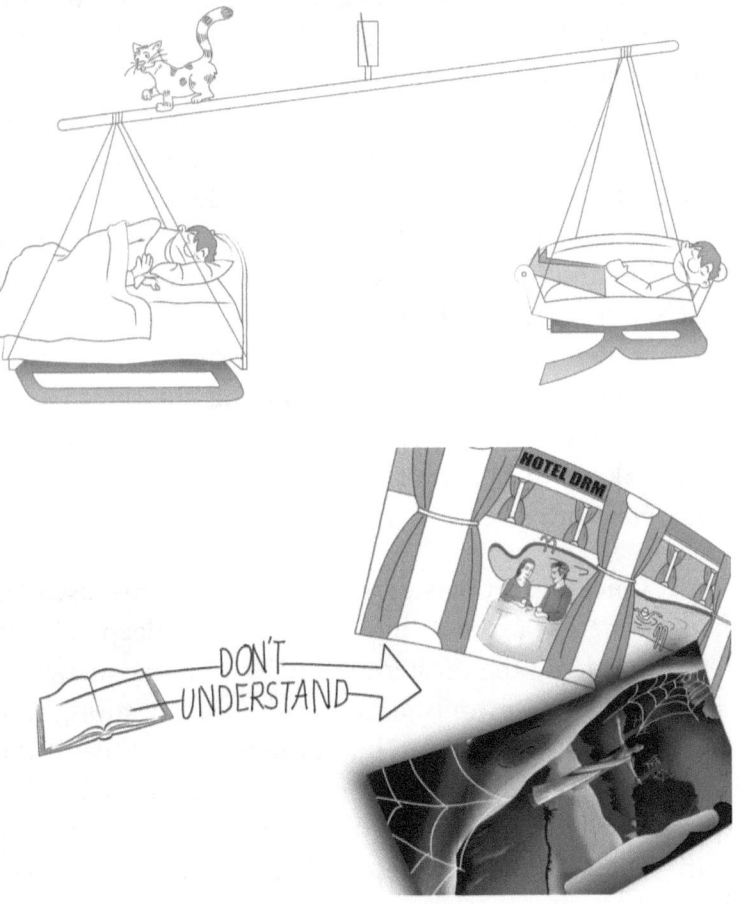

4) One night I went to sleep in my bedroom after finishing one romantic novel. Again I started seeing myself with my eyes closed. My conclusion is that open eyes are a hindrance to seeing oneself. There was a five star hotel and I was on date with a beautiful girl, both of us sitting near swimming pool and enjoying fruit beer. Suddenly when I looked towards the swimming pool, it had changed into a lake. I looked at the pillars of the royal hotel. Those were becoming trees; the curtains had changed into spider webs. We were now in a dense forest. I turned to tell my friend about the change; I saw that her dress had also changed. MeLAN, who was previously wearing jeans and top, was now in a yellow sari and her arms were spread like Kate Winslet (in Titanic) and she was calling me nearer. A terror caught my mind and I came to know that she was not a girl – a witch. I dragged my chair back. She started weeping and her tumbler was full of her tears. Suddenly the tears in her tumbler became red like blood and she threw it on my face. And as I stepped back, I was in the cold waters of the lake. No! I had fallen down from my bed with my body wet with sweat.

2) Once a great master was dying and all his disciples had gathered around him. There was deep silence when suddenly the master asked "Tell me the answer". Everybody was astonished that without question, how could there be an answer, but all kept quiet. One of the disciples gathered courage and said "Sir, what is your question? You haven't asked any question." The master said "Then tell me the question." And in a few moments he died.

5) A young boy was grazing his goats. Some of them were black and some white. An old man was passing from there. He asked the boy – "How much milk do your goats yield?" The boy asked black one or white one. The old man said "Black one". The boy answered – "1 Kg".

The old man asked "And the white?" The boy said "They too yield 1 Kg". The old man again asked – "How much grass do these goats eat in a day?" The boy asked "Black or white?" The old man said "White". The boy answered "2 Kg". The old man asked "And the black one?" The boy said "They too eat 2 Kg". The old man got annoyed and asked the boy why he was asking black one and white one when both ate the same amount of grass and yielded same amount of milk. The boy replied "Actually the black goats belong to my grandfather". The old man said "And the white goats?" The boy replied innocently "They too belong to my grandfather."

9) Two brothers A and B were fighting over who would send the photograph and who would send the parcel to their brother who was working abroad. Suddenly, a man passed by them and asked "What is the name of your brother who is abroad?" A replied – "He is B."

8) A small circle can rotate along the inner circumference of a bigger circle. But can a small square that just fits inside a bigger one rotate along its inner perimeter? No, but a crazy team of 21 people had developed such an instrument (must have used 'Constructive Destruction' type of thing) and their Head was demonstrating it to the Chief of the Institute. It was a prototype and it required a strip of cloth to start the movement. Due to some technical problem it stopped and the situation became awkward. The demonstration was going on beside a place of worship where people were offering prayer to God with gentlemen wearing turbans. One of the 21 members named C had a turban on his head. He rushed towards the window of the worship place and pulled out the turban from the head of a person dissolved in his prayers and started the wonderful machine. The chief asked "Who's turban have you used because you are the only person with a turban and

your turban is on your head." C replied enthusiastically "I pulled it from C's head who is worshipping there." The chief was not astonished because the event was of the year 2057. He understood that this C was not that C.

6) Once I had a muscle rupture and I visited a doctor, who was a boxer too. His whole body was covered with wounds and injuries. The doctor very soon and very excellently fixed my problem, medicated and bandaged my hand. I thanked him and asked when I should revisit him. The boxer (or doctor) replied there was no need for revisit as whenever latest updates would be available or whenever I needed further medication; he would remotely update my medicated band. An excellent example of telemedicine!

Now I STOP.

Now certain questions would be springing up in your mind, but never mind. My mind is also full of questions – "Why did C pull the turban of 'NOT THAT C' and not of other fellow worshippers? Why were A and B fighting? Who was dead – my friend or my friend's brother or may be my brother's friend?" Don't ask for answers, because my head and hand are still aching, not because of muscle rupture but because of so much nonsense and continuous typing. And I am waiting for a medical update from my utopian doctor.

You don't mind. My best wishes that my illogical LOGIC may not exhaust your brains.

Virtually REAL!
Happy Dreaming..., Happy Reading.......

Live Love Dream Laugh

Chapter Eight

Aum

इक ओंकार सतनाम्

Omityekakshar-brahma: AUM is the one letter Big-Bang (Universal Sound) or BRAHMA-NAAD. Those who could know the brahma, heard this universal sound 'AUM' and declared that 'AUM' is the brahma. In reality 'AUM' is neither a letter – because 'AUM' is not included in alphabets of any language; nor 'AUM' is brahma – rather 'AUM' is the sound produced by brahma – the BRAHMA-NAAD. If seen deeply 'AUM' is not even a sound. Because how can brahma alone produce sound; for sound two must collide. Actually language has its limits because of which words, while expressing truth, hide the same under cover. Truth gets polluted by words, imagination and poetry. But for those who have known truth, this is not pollution but beautification of truth. For them '*Omityekakshar-brahma*' is the beautified form of truth.

What is AUM if it is not a sound? Is AUM silence – ultimate silence? No, AUM is not even silence. We only know sound and silence because our music is produced by the combination of sound and silence. But the omnipresent music of AUM is produced by brahma instead of sound and silence. AUM is beyond sound and silence both; is unbeaten drum. Zen monks used to tell their disciples, "*If you want to know the ultimate truth, listen to the clapping of one hand*" – they pointed to this unbeaten drum only, whose beats are not produced by collision of two things. AUM is the '*one hand's clap*'. It is the threshold between sound and silence as virus is the threshold between the living and the non-living. Virus is neither living nor non-living. If it finds some living being, then it resurrects and if it doesn't find one, it remains lifeless. Virus, if enters some living being, becomes alive and if it is preserved in some bottle, it remains lifeless for years. In the same way, AUM, if gets a listener, is a sound and if there is no listener, it is a deep silence.

ॐ *शान्ति, शान्ति, शान्ति !!!*

The extent of AUM can be predicted by the fact that it is not a word of any particular religion or language. In the orient, those Hindus, Jains and Buddhists who attained brahma, heard it and in the west, the enlightened ones of Islam, Judaism and Christianity, heard it. Everyone must have heard the sound alike, but the problem with sound is that everybody cannot pronounce it correctly, and writing it, is even more difficult. There are some people who can utter various sounds like that of a train, a flute etc. But still writing these sounds is very difficult. In Hindi, we write the sound of train as *chhuk-chhuk*, heartbeat as *dhak-dhak*, and that of a bell as *tan-tan*; while in English we write these sounds in a different way. English heart beats as *lubb-dubb* and their bells ring as *tring-tring*. This interpretation and expression of sounds is not correct but our own different approximations. The western religions wrote that always-present sound as 'AMEN'; while the wise men of the east pronounced it as 'AUM'. They also knew that it is impossible to pack natural sounds into letters or words; therefore they discovered a different symbol for this divine sound – ॐ, which was not an alphabet. If the sound of AUM, i.e. *Omkar* is broken, three letters – 'a', 'u' and 'm' emanate from it, which are the three basic sounds and by their combination all sounds can be produced. As white colour breaks into three colours – *Red*, *Green* and *Blue* and their combinations in different proportions can produce all the colours. That means white colour contains all the colours in it. In the same way, Aum contains all the sounds inside it. Aum is that Gangotri from where the Ganges of sounds originates; even silence originates from Aum. That's why when we use Aum before any sentence or *mantra*, its meaning remains the same; rather it gets connected to its source. And Aum is that ocean which drinks and destroys the Ganges of sounds; extincts all sounds by making them fall into silence. That is why we say "*AUM SHANTI*" – although there is no need to add *shanti* (peace) after Aum, because Aum is already an ocean of peace where all sounds are falling and disappearing. But the problem with language is that it creates beauty (*Aum Shanti*) at the cost of truth. Words can never express peace because words break peace.

Aum has touched not only religions, but languages also. There are some words in English language – '*Omniscient*', '*Omnipotent*', and '*Omnipresent*'. If English linguists are asked about their meanings, they are able to tell their meanings – '*seer of all*', '*almighty*', and '*present everywhere*', but they can't tell their root – from where these branched out. Actually these words are made from AUM – Omniscient: *one who saw 'AUM'*; Omnipotent: *one who got the same energy as 'AUM' has*; Omnipresent: *one who appeared in 'AUM'*.

Yogis consider sound as the basic element of existence; while scientists consider electricity as the basic element. Scientists have demonstrated the transformation of electricity into sound; but yogi says that *Omkar* electrifies life force of the body, raises the *kundalini*. Both are correct because both sound and electricity are transformation of a third mysterious element. The same unknowable produces *omkar* – the sound of Aum, the electricity of Aum, which spreads in the whole existence and is heard when, if translated into words, God-Realization happens. Actually calling it God-Realization is not appropriate because God-Realization is too small to express the vast experience of **godliness**. When godliness is experienced, then there is not only vision of God, He is also heard, His fragrance touches the breaths, His electricity touches the body; and His taste touches the tongue too. Because we use our eyes the most, it is called vision – vision of giant sun or a point of light. But the so-called God-Realization is a vast experience, when such experiences also occur which the sense organs are unable to experience. Hearing of *Omkar* is a part of that greatest and ultimate experience.

Because both mind and thought survive on meaning, a thought arises in the mind – what is the meaning of AUM? Aum is not a word; it is sound and what can be the meaning of sound? You can fill any meaning in that sound; in the same way as different languages fill different meanings in the same sound or word. Aum is a *mantra*, which shows meaninglessness to both mind and thought by making them wordless. And mind and thought both die after encountering meaninglessness. To destroy the mind and hence the thought, is the job of *mantra*.

Aum has no meaning or it can be said that all meanings, all words belong to Aum. Aum supports all meanings; has covered all meanings, all words by surrounding them. Aum is the root of all meanings and connects them to meaninglessness.

ॐ मणि पद्मे हुम्

Existence is calling continuously; being a mother, is waking you up, but you are deep asleep and dreaming that you are awake. You are lost in such a way, in deep and long dream of your false reality that you are hearing those sounds, which don't exist. From dream you wake up and soon know that you were in dream. You think you have come back to reality as you wake up. But you don't know that the dream you were seeing inside the dream of '*your reality*' has broken but the long and deep dream of what you consider reality, has not yet broken. But the day you wake up from the dream of what seems to be reality – it is difficult, you reach AUM or in other words, Aum wakes you up from your pseudo-reality and you achieve eternity, where both appearing and occurring events – the pair of dream and reality vanish.

Aum is the call of existence, as if existence wants to show you its miracle, its beauty. Aum is an invitation to take a dive into the ocean of mystery by waking up from deep sleep of your life.

Can we hear 'AUM'? Certainly! Even a deaf can hear; because to listen to Aum, not the ears rather consciousness – totality of consciousness is needed. Then you stand beside a tree, you will hear *omkar* echoing from the tree; you sit near a stone or a rock – the chant of Aum is happening in whole existence. You pay attention to your body – its electricity is converting into Aum – each cell of your body is chanting Aum. And the day you get acquainted to this miracle and beauty, you give up chanting Aum from your throat because you have listened to that deep '*Real Aum*' which comes from your soul; as you extinguish your lamp after seeing the full moon peeping from your window. And even if you don't blow it off, moon's light makes it dim.

The Aum that you chant and all your *mantras* are swallowed by the vast ocean of real Aum, as a river is no more after reaching the ocean. On that day, all your words lose their meanings – the bridge of words between You and the Truth breaks; and Truth and You become one. Then you come to know that *truth* is not different from you, for you to listen to it. After drowning yourself into deep silence, you too become '*silence*'; all your questions disappear, because now you have known that truth is not an answer that you can express after converting it into meanings. Aum ends your journey and opening like a door, points towards a new path. A new journey begins in which you become the journey, the traveller, the path and the destination altogether.

आमीन *!!!*

Happy ॐ!
Happy Listening!!
Happy Reading!!!

Chapter Nine

Self

The promises of this world are, for the most part, vain phantoms; and to confide in one's Self, and become something of worth and value is the best and safest course.

— Michelangelo

First I thought to write about the devilish incident on *16 December 2012* that took place in Delhi but then stopped myself, as so much has been written and said about it. Sometimes unexpected statements were heard from the not-ordinary ones, but the reactions from common person were quite justified. Because it is always the common person who suffers, hence he can be the most authentic.

My understanding is that writing about the incident won't help; it is not going to reverse anything. Rather quantum change in the inner-self, the family, the society and the bureaucracy is needed so that such sinful incidents against *shaktis* don't occur in future. Also

I felt it is not good to scratch the wounds of past. It just saddens us and prevents from sowing new seeds, which can bloom into beautiful and fragrant flowers.

Hence I chose different topic and hope it compensates for what could have been said about the previous one. After all everything is related and an understanding reader can decipher what the writer actually wants to say, whichever topic and language he chooses; whether he uses words from dictionary or his own slang. Feelings expressed by the writer remain the same and alteration of words does not alter the meaning he wants to convey.

Somewhere I write '*you*'; somewhere '*we*' and sometimes I say '*one*' but in all the cases I mean '**WE**'. Sometimes I condemn directly; somewhere I am sarcastic and somewhere humorous and entertaining but every time I am being creative. '*Otherish*' is not a word, but I trust you will get what I mean by it. *Hope I make myself understandable and am forgiven.*

The greatest hazard of all, losing one's self, can occur very quietly in the world, as if it were nothing at all. No other loss can occur so quietly; any other loss – an arm, a leg, five dollars, a wife, etc. – is sure to be noticed.

— Søren Kierkegaard

Is it selfish to be selfish?
Whatever; but *Selfishness leads to SELF*.......

If you are not selfish, then what will you do? You will serve. And you will do it without trying to know whether the other needs your service or not. Almost everyone is on a hunt to serve, trying to find someone who is innocent, smaller or is in trouble, so that one can take him into the trap of his service. Everybody is serving, but nobody is getting served. Service industry is there with so many complaints against it in customer care and consumer forums. Parents and teachers think they are serving the society by producing best human resource as sons, daughters and students; still the society is full of anarchy, unrest and complaints.

All these missionaries, having great passion for service keep searching for the poor and the exploited. The chaos, the complaints and the corruption in society generate work for them. Their obsession is so high that if they fail to find needy people or a chaotic environment, and chances are growing as the world is becoming richer, healthier and happier; they become frustrated and start creating misery so that their mission can continue.

Your service is your way of enslaving the other, dominating the other. Or you burden the other so much with the dues of your service that the other takes revenge. Service should melt you but it increases your ego. Your service is just to divert yourself from your unhappiness and to find that the other is not happier than you. You are not happy, how can you make the other happy. Love yourself, and then only you can love the other. *Be a little selfish...*

Your service is also your strategy to keep yourself engaged. You have made service a job, as sex-workers have made love a profession. In love money is not involved, nor the body – only heart and mind. In the same way service should be spontaneous, not a hunt or mission. Hunting for service comes not from good intentions, and advertising your service is irreligious. Those who advertise and hunt for service, often fail when there is real need of service. These people are only prepared for planned service. As you can't love without a purpose, they can't serve without planning and coverage of their service. *Don't be so much otherish....*

Service should come from our being. This can happen only when we are selfish – we have to start from the self, from where we are. Service should not be a method of increasing our ego. But we are so much interested in enlarging our ego, that to give it a collective shape and mass support, we create a religion out of our investment in service. Without knowing what religion is, we start discovering cheap, mundane and appealing methods to initiate people into what we think religion is and as a result, our service takes a bigger leap into another foolishness of not being in, with the self, but getting lost, out in the shadows and darkness of ego.

People can be easily gathered and the more they are, the bigger we become. When we are over with our service, people can be pulled by projecting their pride on age-old cultural heritage, full of values, simplicity and sacrifice. Nobody thinks that all this appeal of going back to the basics and past is not going to help. One should always look to the present – what we are today and why we are that way? Maybe because we are too much attached to what was suitable and worthwhile for the past and is not so now. We have ovens today, then why bake on fire? We can't follow old primitive lifestyle now. All this is to divert your attention from you and the real problems you are in. But we find good arguments and quotes from our old texts to revert back to old lifestyle. Rather than looking at the past and singing about it and glorifying it, we should improve our present and plan our future, which can never be like our past. Time always needs new. It doesn't permit the old; it welcomes freshness. So we need to be more innovative rather than being repetitive, to enrich and update our heritage. However golden or good it was, history shouldn't repeat because there is always scope for betterment. If we want to repeat our past in future, that means our brains and hearts are dead, and we are worshiping corpses. Our future would be stale and will stink, if it remains past.

Condemnation also attracts, everyone is so much eager to condemn. We can easily gather for that, and never fall short of time. Condemn East, condemn West, and condemn this and that. Why don't we condemn condemnation itself? Religions are woven around condemnation – condemn pleasure, declare it sin; and people who can't relax and live in pleasure will immediately gather. They get a mission of improving others. To improve others, we have to design some exercises for them, which we are not sure would work or not. We insist others to donate, not to tell lies, so on and so forth. Now are we servicing or asking the other to serve us? Have you ever seen anyone who is interested in telling the truth? Rather everyone is trying to prevent others from telling lies. Because everyone knows there is no benefit in truth and if there is some benefit in something, nobody would tell or advertise it. You never tell your neighbour about any profitable purchase or rarely available best stuff in market. You try to hide. Then why do you tell them about virtues and qualities? Because you know these are not virtues, but curses and chains to control the other. *Don't be so much otherish....Be a little selfish...Become better!*

Religions and cultures are not produced or created, forced or repeated; these grow out of our growth – growth of our wisdom. But what we advertise as religion and make our mission is just to create hatred and division under the umbrella of good names like values, virtues, culture and golden past. Religion is not a subject matter of advertisement; and if something becomes mission, it is irreligious.

We don't realize that, somewhere within us all, there does exist a supreme self who is eternally at peace.

— Elizabeth Gilbert

Being selfish is being in the self – connecting with oneself. Every connection needs two ends. Without connecting to yourself, you can't connect to the other and without connecting to the other, you can't know his needs, how will you fulfill those. You will fulfill your own desires in the name of others.

If you think you can connect to the other without connecting to yourself, then that connection would only be physical or superficial. Your minds and hearts will never connect and any connection without the self in it is a sin, in which you are involving the other too. *Be a little selfish*...

Upanishad says everyone is selfish by nature; every act of yours is selfish, it can't be otherwise. Even your trying to be unselfish is out of your selfishness. You breathe for yourself. But you pretend to be unselfish and also present yourselves as practicing charity. This is hypocrisy. Being selfish is the first step towards real charity. When you are totally fulfilled, then only you can fulfill the other. Then only you can help and guide the other without your vested interests in your care.

Otherwise your care won't be in balance and can misguide the other, can even snatch away one's space and freedom. Some parents care too much and that only harms their children rather than helping them. It retards their growth and intelligence. Too much care can be taken only for a short term. Such short-term care is not good for your child and won't help him in the long-term because it will make him handicap. It will make him limp and later he would never stand on his feet and face life. If you really want to care for someone and are really his well-wisher, you will teach him selfishness, so that he may learn how to be independent. Why give someone walking stick when one can be prepared to walk? But you want to make others dependent on you, because you are *otherish* and don't want to lose importance. *Don't be so much otherish....*

I know a girl – her mother was so caring that she could never get space to be herself. Ultimately she escaped her mother, and travelled all around the country, trying to find her own space and freedom. The mother was left behind, but her shadow still chased her. Once it so happened that one of her friends had to go too close to her, trespassing her space. She couldn't tolerate the touch of friend's hair on her face and slapped that girl. Later she realized what she had done. And when she told the whole story, we could understand that she had actually slapped her mother for violating her intimate zone. After one year of being away from home, when it was time for her to return, she was feeling sad.

Caring for others is good, but it should not disturb their peace and should not attack their freedom and dignity. If someone is escaping your care, your care is not care. Beware and care for yourself. Give yourself time. *Be a little selfish...*

What care can you take and how will you know it is comforting the other? You are feeling cold; you will suffocate your child with heavy clothes without knowing that his body is now separate from yours. He has his own intelligence now. Let him use it. You don't overwork. When you work too much, you start doing wrong because right jobs are very few. You start doing things before time or you start doing things that happen on their own.

Selfishness is all about centering into the self, then expanding the self and merging all – rocks, trees, birds, animals and other human beings into the self, thus achieving oneness with all so that your wellness becomes the wellness of all. *Other* doesn't remain, it dissolves into you. The idea of selfish-unselfish is also absorbed into bigger selfishness, because there is no need of being unselfish and hence also of being selfish, as only one '*Self*' remains. But if you are not comfortable with one '*Self*' then you can keep the other as *other*. But then also your selfishness becomes charity, when it falls on the other. You love yourself, you love the other. For the first time you build the real character, where love becomes your art of living.

But your love arises from your mental sickness that makes the other sick too. Love that originates from the '*Self*' is a great healing force, if not forced on the other. But you throw it as bait. You use love as a tool to dominate, control and conquer the other. *Don't be so much otherish....*

We have to dare to be ourselves, however frightening or strange that self may prove to be.
— May Sarton

We don't know what selfish-unselfish is? We don't know what corruption is and we oppose it. We don't know the meanings of words and we start using them and act on them. Actually we don't want to know, because otherwise we would have to go against ourselves.

Even if one is selfish in the sense you think selfishness is, and you are bothered about, then you are more selfish than him. Who are you to judge? Who has given you the authority? His selfishness should not be your concern, if he is not harming you. If it is so, check your intentions; you can't say you are on an improvement campaign and you can't give it a good name as service of humanity. If you want to bring a revolution of betterment, improve yourself; make yourself selfish in becoming uncorrupt, because you can't eliminate others' corruption. For centuries, people are doing that – cleaning others' houses and the dirt, the corruption is as such. Because you are not uprooting its root, that is embedded deep inside you and everybody is so unaware that he can't see the corruption hidden inside himself and propagating from there. Move in. *Be a little selfish...*

People say they never tell a lie and this is the greatest lie, one can tell. Do you know when you tell a lie, you become unconscious first? How can you keep track or count your lies, when you are deep asleep?

It is often the opposite; the selfish person attacks the other and declares him selfish. Parents say that children are selfish without remembering who produced whom. Why did you produce them – so that there is someone to serve you, care for you? It is your selfishness. You take care of them but with a show-off. Your care is not care; it is your investment. You teach them care as a lesson. Care is love, not lesson or investment. Your advice, words, teachings are out of your selfishness.

You limit your service to family, race, region and country and convert it into fight against others. Your service to your people is not out of your love, but because of hatred towards others. *Don't be so much otherish....*

Your type of selfishness can't stand, cooperation is necessary. Today's world is a corporate world; it is taking the shape of global village. The race between tortoise and rabbit of today has totally changed, because the track is different – there is water also. Both of them cooperate and win. When there is land, rabbit takes the tortoise on his back and runs fast, to compensate for when it is tortoise's turn in water and the tortoise swims with rabbit on its back. Now your selfishness won't do, nor your service would do because now all are becoming equal, the difference is of abilities and expertise. In such a scenario, mutual cooperation is the only mantra to achieve success. Today business is running on same principles.

There were two beggars – one lame and the other blind, always competing to get more profit. God thought of doing justice by making them equal. He appeared and asked them for boon, hoping that they would ask to fulfill their deficiencies. But the opposite happened. Lame asked, "Make my rival lame too." And the blind begged God to take away lame man's eyes. You don't be so foolish. Harness your intelligence. Fulfill yourself, whenever there is opportunity. *Don't be so much otherish....*

To equal someone, whose house is in lights we don't light our house; rather we are interested in blowing away his lights. Light your house! *Be a little selfish...*

Learn selfishness to target your always happy SELF...

Happy Lead!
Happy Reading!!

Chapter Ten

Love

Love's conqueror is he whom love conquers.
— Hakim Sanai

Someone is in love and that 'someone' has requested me to write on 'Love'. I know, and feel that the person understands too, that love is a language without any script. It can only be heard, felt, experienced and communicated but not written or read. Words are too dry to contain this juicy nectar. Like a geometrical point it cannot be drawn on paper. As soon as it is written, it vanishes and the reader finds as if something has been rubbed away from the paper.

In all poetry, prose, novels and love-stories love appears as an absence rather than as a presence. It can only be known through living it, then why am I writing about it? Because I also know that absence of something points to its presence. So those who have lived in love may discover it – not in my words but in the absence or gaps between my words and sentences; and will feel its fragrance rising from the paper. And for those who had never been in love till now, my write-up may generate curiosity; and encourage them to give it a try. So let me try the impossible, but the beautiful. If I could create the nostalgia and the curiosity, I would think I had been successful. If I fail, the readers and the requester are free to think that I had never been in love.

Love starts, stays and then keeps increasing. It starts from the self (self or auto-love), progresses to love for the like (homo-love), then reaches love for the different or unlike (hetero-love) and finally expands to love for all, the whole, the universe (universal love). There is yet another life cycle of love beginning from affection (love towards the younger), romance (love towards buddies), trust (love towards elders or higher beings) and ending at devotion ('just love' or love towards none or whole).

Can't you see that the Earth is in love with the Sun and the Sun is in love with the Earth and other planets? The whole universe is a great romance. The immovable rocks, the flowing river, the mighty mountains and the deep blue seas – all are in love. The blooming flowers, the humming bees, the chirping birds, the tall trees and the green grass – all are products of love. Love is quite creative; love is creativity. Love is the source and centre of creation. Rather love is both the creation and the creator.

But nothing is comparable to love between two human beings. The whole existence gets fulfilled when two humans overflow with love and share it. And the two humans too don't remain the same ordinary persons but acquire super-humanity, extraordinariness and beauty. Though in two bodies they become one, however far apart. Not only they become one, the whole nature becomes one with them. Their words dissolve into silence, their eyes start speaking, their bodies acquire grace and they feel more like energies than physical bodies. They think less and feel more; and whatever they do is full of creativity, beauty and benevolence.

Life looks complete, yet always about to complete. There is a change and rise in their quality of life. They become more interested in sharing and giving, than in taking. And if they ever take, they try to gain from existence; and drink and dissolve into the mysteries of nature. Life becomes a beautiful wait and pleasing thirst for something unprecedented and ceases to be a confused run. All ideas are full of love, wrapped and centred in love. Mornings are more beautiful and evenings are even more than ever. In loneliness too, the company of the companion is felt and when with the companion, one gets lost. Lovers always discover a new world more explorable than the existing one. The more they explore the more newness their world acquires. And this exploring continues and never tires them. Love never dies. It never ends to completion.

Love is a multidimensional phenomenon that starts with oneself and then propagates like oceanic waves in all directions beyond time and space. It bridges life and death. Love is not an act but a happening – a pure experience. It can't be done, rather it is the doer. It does a lot to the lovers; it completes them and keeps completing them. Sometimes it looks like a fall; at others it is a rising. It is a journey from ego to soul, from mind to the heart, from man to woman, from lust to prayer and from sex to God. Love takes you from selfishness to altruism. Love is like rising and falling breaths or waves; the lubb-dubb of the heart – an energy phenomenon converting rigidity into flexibility; and melting the expansion of time into a drop of moment.

Is love out of need or the ultimate need? The question remains unanswered. But it can be said that love is the basic, inherent and the greatest need of life – love is life itself or very near. That depends on the psychology of man and woman. In my understanding, love is subset of life for a man but for a woman life is a subset of love and the resultant of the two views combined together makes love equivalent or synonymous to life. It can't be out of need because then it becomes conditional and conditional love is not love.

Other needs can be postponed – even breath can be held for some time – but the need for love can't be. It is such a necessity that a single moment of absence can be fatal. Even the cruelest person cannot survive without love. His love may have chosen wrong objects like power, money etc. or may have become distorted as lust and sex.

One has to have some passion to live. Passion dies, the person dies. A child's passion for his teddy bear and a youth's passion for his mobile are also forms of love. Love is an insatiable fulfillment.

Love is a flow – a current of energy. The more it overflows, the more the liveliness. When this flow stops, the stagnation of energy becomes hatred. Unexpressed love also becomes poisonous. Since energy is still there, a person can live by hatred too. In flow also, there are infinitesimal moments or sometimes longer durations of halt i.e. hatred. Hence love co-exists with hatred. Therefore all relations are love-hate relationships. Love is like light or an electric lamp which appears to throw light; but actually it throws darkness also, fifty times in a second. But we see only light. That means light also contains or hides darkness in it. Similarly love is so vast and acceptive that it comprehends and contains hatred too – its very opposite.

If you judge people, you have no time to love them.

— Mother Teresa

*The only condition in love is that... it is unconditional....it is bound to be unbounded.......
Relationships are not.*

— Author

Some people mistakenly consider attachment as love but it is not; rather it is absence of love. Attachment is, when your love dries and no more flows, the love energy converting into clinging to one; when you start giving more importance to the object of love than love itself. Love is a multi-directional overflowing and when the flow stops, it becomes ego, jealousy, possessiveness and lust. Love makes you a master; as nobody, not even your mind can stop you from loving. But most people oppose, repress and divert it or try to bind and encage it. They end-up becoming slaves themselves.

Love breathes in freedom like life breathes in oxygen. Without freedom, one can't love. That's why most marriages, even love marriages, destroy love; as freedom is gone. Love is a flying bird, not an encaged one. Love makes one fearless. Love and fear can't co-exist. If someone is full of fear, anxiety and depression, introduce him/her to love or introduce love to him/her. All negativities would disappear. Love is medicine; love is cure and the greatest healer in the world.

To escape the chaos and dynamism created by love, society has introduced artificial love. Society becomes a third party and tries to keep a control over love. This has resulted in, love getting associated with guilt. Because of fear, we rarely find people in love; and what seems to us as love is nothing, but a seeking for a match or partner in life to cope with its difficulties, and live smoothly. Those people who dare to love, have either to go against society or they love secretly as if it were a crime or sin; and hence nobody is benefitted by love because of guilt. Lack of love is the reason behind so much exploitation, violence and lust seen in present generation. Love is being used for exploitation, violence and slavery, and to satisfy lust.

Love is your very breath; your being. Without it you become a machine. Society, priests and politicians killed the great sage of love – Saint Valentine. They are successful in deceiving people and replacing love, very cleverly with bondage – something very artificial to resemble and substitute it. And they have created rules of love and have given birth to so many myths about it. Love is illogical and without rules; and they have made it a mental phenomenon, writing books, scriptures and poetry not about it, but the rules. Love as a practice has disappeared from life, while love is a practical stuff rather than being a theoretical concept.

Then there are scientists and logicians who have made love a chemical phenomenon. They say it is a madness, blindness and stupidity occurring because of release of some hormones like oxytocin in the blood. No! Love originates from the heart and is the cause of release of those hormones, which bring ecstasy to a person. Yes! Love is blind, but that blindness is very beautiful; as in that darkness things become crystal clear.

Love is the greatest culture, but the society thinks that their culture is at risk, when it finds two persons holding hands with love. Love never knows three, it ends up at two and a half – two lovers and half their love; half, because it never reaches completion and always seeks perfection. Hence there is no place for courts, priests-popes, parents-gurus and not even God as a third person trying to govern it. And when love intensifies, that 2.5 becomes one; as the lovers disappear and only pure love remains. Love is very personal; it is meditation when directed towards oneself. It is actually YOU; then how can there be any scope for the other to come in between to tie a knot. No ritual is needed as an initiation of love; love initiates itself – when and how, nobody knows. No ritual is greater than love and is rather a barrier to the stream of love. Love knows neither age nor ages. It can span and occur across time and space. Meera's love for Krishna is a testimonial to that.

Love is in the air like fragrance. One can't grab it; it can only be felt. You have to be it because you are made of love; because of love between your parents. Love makes you a devotee and makes your lover/ beloved a god.

The journey of love starts from lust to romance to prayer and ultimately converges to a single point called meditation or we should say love-meditation. Love becomes meditation ultimately and meditation becomes love ultimately because both are a single point – the origin in their ultimate form. When we don't know them, they appear as two separate phenomena far apart, but when we start our journey into any one of them, the other appears as a reflection of the former. As we approach nearer, the distance between the two seems to be decreasing as if the mirror is being brought nearer. Ultimately when we reach our destination of love or meditation and totally dissolve into it, we find that we were the mirror that was making them two. It was a single phenomenon having no name or we can say having two names, the other name given in ignorance, to the reflection through us. As the mirror of ego dissolves, illusion of the two vanishes. Once we have reached that origin, we have reached; rather to say, have become the ultimate (God in layman's term). Then there is nowhere to go. That point of origin itself remains or becomes the journey and the traveller. Lover merges with what he called love and meditator merges with what he called meditation.

Now when this origin expands outside, it becomes love and when it contracts inside, it becomes meditation. Circumference is nothing but expansion of the centre and centre is nothing but intensifying of the circumference. The circle completes. The door is the same – if we exit, love; if we enter, meditation.

Love is the process of becoming and finding the ONE, and that ONE is truth, bliss and awareness. At the lowest and the physical level, love is sex – the seed; and at the highest and spiritual, it becomes God – the ultimate flowering, the beautiful tree. Love is the only spirituality, the only truth; and the ultimate stuff left when nothing remains. That's why love is God.

Love created by beauty is illusion – false; because beauty is temporary and short-lived; while true love creates beauty and that beauty is as true and permanent as love. Everyone is in search of real love when they themselves are unreal, and not ready and mature enough for the conscious romance. Everybody wants love and is not ready to give it.

Love knows no responsibility because love itself is responsibility. To separate love and responsibility is simply stupid.

— Osho

All actions without love are mere duties; all actions performed on others' requests or orders, or by reading and following scriptures are duties and duty is a burden: an ugly word. With love you know how to respond. Love makes you responsible, because it comes from inside. And that which comes from your inner core is not duty; it is responsibility.

Love is a wonderful game consisting of fluctuations, ups and downs, truth and dare, beautiful and well-wished lies. Players change but the game never ends and takes you towards your destiny.

If you want to know more about love, then go to a child; he will tell you what it is, with his hugs and kisses; but go tenderly, go delicately and with respect towards him.

At last, let us perform *purnahuti* (complete surrender or sacrifice) to 'LOVE' with these lines:

> Love is a name, love is game,
> Love is aimless, love is an aim;
> Love is pride, love is shame,
> Love stays on, remains the same.
>
> Love is a rise, love is fall,
> Love is silent, love is a call;
> Love is nothing, love is all.
>
> Love is joy, love is pain,
> Love is loss, love is gain;
> Love is never, love is again.

Love is God, love is religion,
Love is life, love is a relation;
Love is journey, love is a station,
Love stays on; an endless lesson.

Happy Loving!
Happy Reading!!
Love you, Adore you, and Bless you!!!

Chapter Eleven

Time and Limit

The only limit to your impact is your imagination and commitment.

— Tony Robbins

A thought came into my mind to write something on *'time as a byproduct of limit'*. And in no time, I came to know that the thought created a limit. The thought itself was the limit. The boundaries of thought produced time. If there are no boundaries, no partitions and no divisions, then there is no time. Like thought, event also creates time because event can be divided into many. Whenever we divide and lose oneness, time gets created. Moving is a way of dividing the space. The slower we move, the more we divide and the more the time. The faster we move, the less we divide and the lesser the time. If we move with such fast speed that we don't divide space into 'travelled' and 'to travel', then time becomes zero. Space can't move over itself, hence it cannot divide itself and hence space never experiences time. Space is all alone without time. We carry little space and this limit of ours creates time.

Time is a phenomenon of change and change is perceived because of the limit of the mind or journey of the mind on the whole or the event. Because mind proves to be a small window to the scene of the whole and the event, it keeps moving and breaking the event into smaller events and storing them as experiences, thoughts and dreams. This whole activity of mind creates time as a store of events. Whatever creates time is limited, so in all cases limit is the mother of time. Limitlessness means eternity.

Partialness is the limit and partialness is nothing but mind. When a room is viewed through a keyhole, eyes are unable to get the whole view of the room. The keyhole only provides a partial view of the room – sometimes sofa, sometimes television, table etc. and at others this wall and that wall. This limit of the keyhole doesn't let to see the whole room and mind comes into picture to create the whole room out of the viewed pieces through the keyhole. Similar is the case with universe. Universe is the room without any walls. And mind is the keyhole getting different partial views of this room as time.

Universe is the whole without limits. If anything is kept outside the universe, the separation of it from the universe creates boundary and universe ceases to be whole. It becomes a part of something bigger. This is a paradox as it limits the universe and also makes it a part. That thing needs to be included in the universe to keep the universe whole. Now knowing that everything is inside the universe, can we speak of time of universe or age of universe? No, because for that a clock is needed which must be kept outside of the universe and doing so, universe will not remain universe. It must include the clock and if it includes the clock, how can that clock measure its age. To know the displacement of an object, the reference point should be outside the object; if it is inside there is no displacement ever. Hence for the whole or the universe, there is no time. Time is seen only in one part of universe when other part can keep the clock. Time is a phenomenon of relativity in partial universe with respect to other parts of it.

Time is a by-product or an expression of relativity happening inside universe due to space. Time is nothing but the separation of objects in the universe. It is the distance between two bodies in the universe. It is always between two. That two may be anything – objects, events or thoughts. For the one i.e. universe, it is not. Universe is one event and one space without anything outside to create relativity.

When you look at the sky at night and see stars, galaxies and other heavenly bodies; you are observing different times. Speed of light and light year explain it. The distance is so much that the whole scene is past and not one past, but many. The whole sky is not at one time but many. Observed moon is the recent past – some seconds earlier, some bodies are observed as what they were one or two years ago and some galaxies appear in the time of your great, great forefathers. The sun one watches in the morning or at noon is a different time – 8 minutes earlier. When the whole sky is past for you, then you and your Earth must be future for them i.e. other heavenly bodies. Simple relativity!

Scientists say time is a statistical phenomenon like temperature. When there is no molecular motion, temperature is 0 Kelvin. As temperature is generated because of molecular motion or differences in heat, time is generated because of relative motion or distances in space. Like temperature, it doesn't exist physically. The motion may occur outside in space or inside in consciousness. Consciousness becomes mind when there is movement of thoughts in it. Hence mind is consciousness with limits or it is a window to consciousness.

For mind there is time; there is time between two thoughts. For consciousness, there is no time because there is no motion or relativity in it. Mind is the measure of time. Time is measured by mind and it is measured differently. A person goes to sleep at 10 PM and wakes up at 4 AM. Time measured is not always the same. It depends on the activity of the mind, because activities of the mind measure time. If there is no activity during this period, the person may not experience any time. He would experience only two points as 10 PM – the time when he went to sleep and 4 AM – the time when he woke up. The sleep – the separation of two points 10 PM and 4 AM becomes an instant, since there is no measurement in mind. It happened with Rip Van Winkle – Washington Irving's character in primary school story, who got intoxicated on a hill (Kaatskill mountains) and when woke up after twenty years he thought that he had woken up the next morning but found that he had grown too old and the new people in his village did not recognize him.

Time is nature's way of keeping everything from happening at once.
— John Archibald Wheeler

Once we accept our limits, we go beyond them.
— Albert Einstein

Sometimes the opposite happens – one sleeps for half an hour and feels that he has slept for centuries. He might have seen dreams, which have spanned over centuries – a movie featuring many generations. This person has undergone too much mental activity in just half an hour and his mind has hence measured too much time between the sleeping and waking point. This is the phenomenon of mental time, which is zero if there is no thought, dream or mental activity.

Mental time is nothing but the space created by mind through its activity of thought and imagination. It appears because of change and is different from physical time, which appears because of the extension of space, and is infinite. The unit of physical time is the space traversed by light in one year known as the distance of one light year in the universe. Its account is kept by a clock, which also has a uniform speed and it is relatively very small as compared to speed of light. Physical and mental time run differently and seldom match because both have different relativities. One has its relativity in outer space and the other has its relativity in inner space – the mind. Rip Van Winkle experienced these two times so differently – the mental time of one night's sleep and the physical time of twenty years.

Mental time depends on the speed of mind and physical time depends on the speed of light. When one has to wait, time is longer; when one has to reach, time runs faster. In a clock the physical time (its ticking rate) runs uniformly, but it is said that for increasing gravitational force or in faster inertial system, the speed of time measured (measured time) from our place decreases. Thus a person travelling with nearly the speed of light is supposed to return younger than the person staying at our place if both were of same age, and another person of same initial age returns older after a few years' stay on a planet where gravitation is weaker than at our place. In a black hole, gravity is so strong that the speed of time measured from our place almost becomes zero.

A black hole also distorts time. It has an event horizon, a mathematical boundary at the gravitational radius (known as Schwarzschild radius) which defines its size and at which the gravitational pull becomes so great as to make escape impossible, even for light. As a result, nothing can be observed from outside. At the event horizon, time practically stops for the outside observer and events inside the horizon cannot affect him. Anything when crosses this limit called event horizon of the black hole, is assumed to fall towards the centre (known as spacetime singularity) and disappear into 'no-time', to become part of black hole.

After the event horizon is crossed, the spacetime singularity cannot be avoided; hence escape is not possible. Inside the event horizon (known as interior of black hole), time and space swap roles, where future corresponds to decreasing radius. So, the interior is actually in the future compared with the exterior. Anything that is caught by the interior (i.e. future) is prevented from turning around and escape out to the exterior (i.e. past) of balck hole, because it cannot travel to the past. It can only travel towards future, that is towards singularity. Time only goes forwards, never backwards. In fact, it really is time that pulls it towards the singularity at the centre of black hole. Trying to avoid reaching the singularity would be like attempting to halt time.

At the super-galactic scale, time is relative to speed of light, and again science assumes that at the sub-atomic level (scale of 1000 times smaller than the nucleus of hydrogen atom), time exists in a bubbly, foamy character as quantum foam (known as spacetime foam). And I suspect it exists only as expression, relativity or reflection of space. It is supposed that at the sub-atomic scale, time is jittery, constantly turbulent and fluctuates in foam like manner. It consists of many small, ever-changing regions for which space-time are no longer definite.

It is assumed that quantum foam is a network of wormholes and virtual black holes. Predicted by the theory of general relativity, wormholes are tunnel-like connections made out of spacetime, offering a shorter distance between two vastly separated areas of the universe. Through wormholes in spacetime foam, there are also links with all times – past and future, and through virtual black holes, even with parallel universes.

From the discussion above, regarding claims made by science about '*time*', it is indicated that time has different pattern for positions in different gravitational systems, different speeds and different scales. But if we can overcome, transcend and go beyond these differences, and take a dive into consciousness, there is nothing as '*time*' – just an *Eternal NOW* exists.

At the electron level energy exists as probability. Electron itself exists as electron cloud, which is the probability space of its position. Its orbit around the nucleus is not certain and the probable space of its revolution is known as orbital.

It is supposed that the nature or pattern of space too, is such that it exhibits two probabilities – true and false. This prediction internally limits space and snatches away its continuity. The true-false probability gives discreteness to space where its truth has been found to be a chunk or square of 10^{-35} meter, separated or woven by no-space. This shows that space also is an alternating flow and its smallest unit is a chunk of 10^{-35} meter squared.

If you are in a pattern, you are in a limit. This limit, this pattern makes your fate. Bill Gates' fate is to be surrounded by money. He can't avoid it; however he tries, unless he comes out of his mind. Failure is fate;

success is fate. Each person's mind is a limited pattern and the person uses this mind to live his life. This makes his life also a pattern, which is otherwise very vast and random. Pattern of mind makes life seem to be governed by fate. Life becomes a pattern or fate when lived in a limit through mind. Limit, pattern, mind and fate, hence become synonymous. Life is more; it contains all these. Fate is nothing but limit to life imposed by your mind so that you can live it securely. Life is random. Randomness leads to limitlessness or infinity. Life is limitless but lifetime is a limit. When life is seen through time or limit, it gets crystallized as lifetime.

Time is a limit and time is further divided into limits of eras, millenniums, Y2K, 2012... so on and so forth, and then there are controversies. There are great disagreements over the period of eras, their start and end. Even internationally followed Gregorian calendar created confusion whether second millennium ended on 31st December 1999 or 2000. Everybody knows millennium contains 1000 years; that means there is confusion about the start year, about AD and BC; or the start was not proper or arithmetic; or there were too many manipulations – additions and deletions of days, years in the calendar in between. Whatever be the reason mathematics says if thousand sticks are equivalent to a millennium, then 2000 sticks make two millenniums and the third millennium starts with stick number 2001. Counting starts with 1. Zero is not a part of natural numbers and is not used in counting natural things. However it is used in counting indices in certain computer languages.

Boundaries are to protect life, not to limit pleasures.

— Edwin Louis Cole

If you judge people, you have no time to love them.

— Mother Teresa

Computer or IT industry also faced time problem, much talked about as the Y2K problem due to the limit of memory assigned to represent year in Operating Systems and application programs. Due to representation of year with only 2 digits, there was no way to distinguish between 1930 and 2030 and no way to tell that 40 years have passed between 1975 and 2015 and not 60. This confusion to machine was bound to create major errors in various time dependent calculations, especially financial, which could lead to bankruptcy of persons, organizations and even banks.

And then there was another time problem! Will 2013 come? Or the world ends in 2012? As no calendar had been framed for time after 2012 by an old civilization, expert in calendaring time; they might have known the end of world or might have got tired limiting time, which never ends. Old calendars, eras and years end and new ones start. But that's not a big problem. If the world ends tomorrow despite having a date and calendar for tomorrow, it will end. Nobody will ever know, because start and end are not part of time. They are out; they are the limits creating time.

Limit formats eternity into time. Limit formats the universe into space and dimensions. This helps in addressing and communicating space and time. It is again a limit of our senses and instruments that we find the universe limited to 3 dimensions with relativity. Science expects that universe might have at least 10 dimensions and someday these may be caught or perceived; maybe not by senses but by instruments or experiments. But that '10' is again a limit. And all perceptions and experiences are limits as far as the limitless and timeless phenomenon of universe is concerned. These are limits like speed, and more dimensions and more accuracy just means increasing the speed, and not measuring the ultimate. There the journey of science ends.

Pen-ultimately, limit is beautiful and it has its advantages – unlimited advantages. I'll only quote what my limited mind and thoughts can recall and what the limited time available to me permits.

Limit divides and divided may be conquered. Limit captures – all perceptions, experiences and measurements are because of the limit of our senses and instruments. These are the windows that capture, not only capture; but also recreate the scene. The poor universe is un-captured. No limits!

Limit creates; because for creation boundaries are needed. A beautiful painting is created out of the limits of lines and curves. Limit makes life easy; it creates patterns and patterns decorate life. It creates addresses, personalities, variations and seasons, and kills boredom. Limit creates goals, and lets us remember and forget.

Limit produces time – time to toil and time for leisure. Limit produces thoughts – thoughts lead to creativity or destruction for re-creativity. This chapter is a limit and the result of limit, because it needed thoughts and time to write, and it will need the same to read.

Limit starts and limit ends. Limit is rest. Life is not limited, but limit is life.

Ultimately to limit the '*limit*', let us define it:

[*Mathematical definition of limit: A determinate quantity, to which a variable one continually approaches, and may differ from it by less than any given difference, but to which, under the law of variation, the variable can never become exactly equivalent.*

$x \to 0$ means $x \neq 0$ either $x - 0 <$ delta or $0 - x <$ delta

Here 0 is the limit.

For a function which takes a real number and returns another real number, limit is defined in the following way –

limit $f(x)$ = limiting value of $f(x +$ epsilon$)$ as epsilon $\to 0$
$x \to x0$

(that should be value of $f(x0 +$ epsilon$))$. Let this value be L.

Roughly speaking, for values of x "close to" $x0$, the function f gives values "close to" L.]

Why spare 'time':

[*Time: Fourth dimension: the fourth coordinate that is required (along with three spatial dimensions) to specify a physical event.*

Observing a certain number of repetitions of one or another standard cyclical event (such as the passage of a free-swinging pendulum) constitutes one standard unit such as the second.

Time is part of the fundamental structure of the universe, a dimension in which events occur in sequence.

Time does not refer to any kind of "container" that events and objects "move through", nor to any entity that "flows", but that it is instead part of a fundamental intellectual structure (together with space and number) within which humans sequence and compare events.]

I wake up at four to sleep more. If there is no limit, there can't be more. Limit creates the limitless. Limitless is because of the limit.

Men talk of killing time, while time quietly kills them.

— Dion Boucicault

Happy Reading!
But within limits!!
In limitless, you'll lose yourself!!!

Chapter Twelve

Form and Formula

"Form is emptiness, emptiness is form" states *the Heart Sutra, one of the best known ancient Buddhist texts. The essence of all things is emptiness.*

— Eckhart Tolle

I am going to keep this chapter as brief as possible because what I am preaching or better say, pointing here is form, not formula. This chapter is just the form and all elaborations will make the formula.

Form has a permanency whereas formulas die, get transformed, improved or replaced. Form can be preserved while formula are often lost; and then those are revived and rediscovered from the form. This existence is the form – the pure desire or longing, and its vivid expressions as life forms and nature, are the formations.

The sutras, the axioms are all forms – the source from where many explanations, treatises, theorems and formulas flow. Form is the potential or the mother that produces its progeny i.e. the whole creation; and the ultimate mother – the mother of all forms is formless or formlessness. Creation is from formless to form and from form to formula. Form gets formulated to give rise to a formula whose formulation is expressed in the objects of the world.

Form follows function – that has been misunderstood. Form and function should be one, joined in a spiritual union.
— Frank Lloyd Wright

The primary colours – *Red, Green and Blue* are forms and millions of colours produced by their combinations in different proportions are the formula or their formulation.

The real guide gives the form, not formula; then one can create his own formula. One should always try to remember the form; formula are so many. If you have the seed (form), you too have the trees (formula). Form is portable; formula may be not. Form is like torch and formula like map. Maps fail when it is dark.

Songs and compositions are the formula, music is the form. You have to know music and the compositions flow. Guide is the one who indicates or shows the formless by manifesting it into form. He produces music out of silence.

Guide gives you the desire; and your achievements and accomplishments follow when you formulate according to your endeavours.

Every formula of every religion has in this age of reason, to submit to the acid test of reason and universal assent.

— Mahatma Gandhi

Science and man can see only with boundaries and limitations. Limitation of the form is the formula. So they start with such formula, which later they find, were just limiting cases of some general bigger formula. Thus science moves back to the source and reaches the form.

Science starts from matter and finds energy, while existence manifests energy to form matter. Science gropes and discovers so many theories like *general relativity, special relativity, quantum field theory* etc. But every theory proves to be not completely satisfactory for unified description of fundamental law of the universe.

In search of Theory of Everything (**ToE**), new theories keep popping up like *'String Theory', 'superstring theory', 'M-theory', 'bosonic string theory'* etc. No theory proves to be the Theory of Everything and I guess only *'no-theory'* can.

'Can there be a ToE?' is a big question and the answer falls in the realms of mystery, not science. To know how form becomes formula is within the purview of science, but how form emerges from the formless is

out of bounds for science. It is a pure experience, not any theory.

This was the form.

The idea that I presented here is just the form that can later be expanded by the readers into various ideas, principles, doctrines or formulas – both '*for*' and '*against*'.

Formations and compositions will follow.

There's no formula.

— J. K. Rowling

Happy formations and formulations!
Happy Reading!!

Chapter Thirteen

Schrodinger's Cat

Science is not about making predictions or performing experiments. Science is about explaining.

— Bill Gaede

Schrodinger's cat experiment is a thought experiment. One friend has asked me to explain it. I don't know how to explain, as it is self-explanatory.

A cat is in a closed box. Schrodinger says that to the outside universe the cat is dead and alive at the same time. The setup is such that its survival depends on the quantum nature of radioactive decay. There is a Geiger counter inside the box and a radioactive substance in such small quantity that only one atom decays in one hour or even none. If it decays, it empties the Geiger counter; as a result a hammer falls that tumbles a flask containing hydrocyanic acid, resulting in the death of the cat.

Leonardo da Vinci says "*To develop a complete mind: study the science of art; study the art of science. Learn how to see. Realize that everything connects to everything else.*" If you develop this skill, you will find that not only the movement of planets, stars and constellations affect you, but also an event as small as flowering of a bud surely affects you. You know flowering is a bigger event in comparison to decay of an atom, which decides whether a cat will survive or die. Astrology tries to approximate on the basis of a few, large and more contributory intermediaries, and sometimes comes out as a success. But why does it often fail? Because as the cause of any event, there is involvement of all i.e. will of everyone (we can call it the WHOLE) and a single sneeze can affect the chain and change the course. It is going to be a complex calculation.

In January 2001, Stephen Hawking in his Albert Einstein lecture on "*Predicting the future: from astrology to black holes*" at Siri Fort Auditorium, New Delhi indicated that events are uncertain. It is not certain to even find the position of an electron whose area of movement is restricted to an orbital, how can one be certain about bigger things – living things that have so much of freedom.

This experiment extends quantum concepts applied at microscopic levels to macroscopic levels and it is so, but it is difficult for us to find the chain – Geiger counter, radioactive substance, hammer, and hydrocyanic acid. The chain may be much longer and might be spread in the vast extension of space-time, sometimes centuries – too big for our lifespan. The chain may involve uncountable intermediaries.

So if you are reaping something and find there is some injustice; you don't know it was sown by your forefathers and there was all the stuff – the Geiger counter, radioactive substance, hammer etc. that connected you to them and you were in the same closed box unable to jump out. The whole world now is a box though often it is called a global village. If any decay happens in America, the cat dies in India.

See now the power of truth; the same experiment which at first glance seemed to show one thing, when more carefully examined, assures us of the contrary.

— Galileo Galilei

I explained to my friend: you are the cat and you are inside the box. And as long as you are inside the box, there is no difference between life and death. You think you are living but you are already dead. Come out of the box, otherwise the decay is going to happen and the hydrocyanic acid will fall on you. Your life is dependent on your efforts for survival and one day you are going to lose energy; and you don't know of survival without effort.

Listen to Leonardo da Vinci –'*everything is connected*', and the universe is a self-perpetuating machine, which is making all efforts for your survival. You need not make extra efforts because they often go against you, and tumble down the flask of hydrocyanic acid.

Come out of the box of your ambitions, the false ideas, principles, imaginations, expectations and hypotheses you have created by yourself. Claim your freedom by disassociating yourself from all this rubbish. Meditate to come out of the box of rotten mind. The box is death and outside is the only certainty – that is life.

Unrelate yourself by finding the self-love inside you. Don't be a part of this weak chain – Geiger counter and other intermediaries, because this life, dependent on your breath is going to finish after a few counts; the hammer of death is ready to fall and strike your head any time. Find the inner space where there is no death – there you are always alive and there is no hydrocyanic acid there to burn. But certainly an immortal flame of celebration is glowing, which is your real life.

Find out: you are not inside any box, you are part of this vast freedom called life that is certain, flowing amidst all the other uncertainties – of events, wills, efforts, determinations and involvement of others. These all are death prone.

Explore, Experiment, Evolve.
                                        — Lailah Gifty Akita

Happy Understanding!
Happy moving out of the box of darkness to the infinite space of light...

Epilogue

"We may seem to be a structure from outside but from inside we are much more – a helix of revolution."

Chapter One – **"Change"**

"Before doing any act to the other, put yourself in his place."

Chapter Two – **"Gandhi"**

"Rise beyond all divides so that you can raise your fellows to feel what pleasure it gives. And if you've really risen, you will certainly raise so that there is someone on your grounds to race with you so that you reach your Goal of Excellence as the best record."

Chapter Three – **"Rise"**

"My message for the students and learners is to minimize on probability and maximize on potential so that the possibility of success gets optimized. You are born to succeed and achieve. Success and achievement are your potential; you just have to harness them. Don't make them

probabilities by studying and not learning. Learn and experiment to open up the possibilities of understanding and experience."

Chapter Four – **"Study"**

"Whenever you encounter communal problems, don't fan the fire; don't initiate or support rumours. Instead try to dig out whose personal interests are initiating the madness. Understand, explain the real cause, educate people and hit at the root."

Chapter Five – **"Community Crysis"**

"The group should be committed to harness the creativity and thrill of the wonderful persons who constitute it. It should welcome innovative ideas and the quality of sharing, and provide help to its members. It should be an open forum for mutual advice, counselling and information interchange."

Chapter Six – **"Interest Group"**

"Un-understand."

Chapter Seven – **"Don't Understand"**

"aum mani padme hum."

Chapter Eight – **"Aum"**

"Selfishness is all about centering into the self, then expanding the self and merging all – rocks, trees, birds, animals and other human beings into the self, thus achieving oneness with all so that your wellness becomes the wellness of all.

Other doesn't remain, it dissolves into you. The idea of selfish-unselfish is also absorbed into bigger selfishness, because there is no need of being unselfish and hence also of being selfish, as only one 'Self' remains. But if you are not comfortable with one 'Self' then you can keep the other as other. But then also your selfishness becomes charity, when it falls on the other. You love yourself, you love the other. For the first time you build the real character, where love becomes your art of living."

Chapter Nine – "**Self**"

"Love you... Adore you.... And Bless you......."
Chapter Ten – "**Love**"

"Limit produces time – time to toil and time for leisure. Limit produces thoughts – thoughts lead to creativity or destruction for re-creativity. This chapter is a limit and the result of limit, because it needed thoughts and time to write, and it will need the same to read."

Chapter Eleven – "**Time and Limit**"

"Form has a permanency whereas formulas die, get transformed, improved or replaced. Form can be preserved while formula are often lost; and then those are revived and rediscovered from the form. This existence is the form – the pure desire or longing, and its vivid expressions as life forms and nature, are the formations."

Chapter Twelve – "**Form and Formula**"

"*A cat is in a closed box. Schrodinger says that to the outside universe the cat is dead and alive at the same time. The setup is such that its survival depends on the quantum nature of radioactive decay. There is a Geiger counter inside the box and a radioactive substance in such small quantity that only one atom decays in one hour or even none. If it decays, it empties the Geiger counter; as a result a hammer falls that tumbles a flask containing hydrocyanic acid, resulting in the death of the cat.*"

Chapter Thirteen – "**Schrodinger's Cat**"

Happy moving out of the box of darkness to the infinite space of light...

AMEN!

Understood / Not Understood

READER

About the Author

"The pioneer person may be invisible because 'Wonders occur when the person becomes invisible and his ideas start becoming visible'. The source of all ideas is Nature's Intellect; ideas just land on some mind – ready to receive and accept."

From Chapter Six – "**INTEREST GROUP**"

The artist, the creator must be invisible; then only can he create something of worth. All creations occur in utter darkness. A seed has to remain buried deep inside the darkness of the soil; a baby has to pass through nine months of darkness inside the womb of its mother.

The greatest Creator GOD, himself is invisible.

Author is also a creator who creates with pen, an artist who plays with words and puts them to dance.

All authors are great observers and if the observer is hidden, the events don't get interfered by his presence.

Like guide (guru) and God, author is also single consciousness that manifests itself in some blessed ones. Vyaas (व्यास) is the Indian name for the authority to write. Author belongs to the universal.

Like all artists, authors including this one are sensitive, expressive and might know the art of saying certain things by not saying them.

You can see the courage shown in this creative work by being indifferent to whether others understand or not. Real authors are mostly fearless and welcome all types of comments and criticism.

Authors write to achieve satisfaction, to share and convey what they have in their hearts, but remain dissatisfied that they couldn't say it all. Something always remains unsaid. Like lovers, they feel the pain that something was left or missed or not fully expressed.

That which remains unsaid belongs to poetry and becomes mythology.

Sometimes, it may also happen that existence speaks through them; their words seem to contain God's love, grace, wisdom and intelligence.

Author has great responsibility to disseminate his findings and experiences from nature, books and teachers for providing healthy food for the minds of those who are thirsty to learn and want to exercise their brains. Author is like a guardian to the readers.

He may even heal some readers, motivate, encourage and inspire them.

This author is not an exception. He is a channel to healing force also.

He loves you... adores you.... and blesses you.......

To know and explore what is different in him:

Keep connected @ facebook: /totally.TOTAL
Interact: paresh.bhandari@gmail.com